The Brief and True Report of

Temperance Flowerdew

A Novel

The Brief and True Report of
Temperance Flowerdew

A Novel

Denise Heinze

BLACK
STONE
PUBLISHING

Published in 2020 by Blackstone Publishing
Cover and book design by Zena Kanes

Printed in the United States of America

First edition: 2020
ISBN 978-1-982598-64-8
Fiction / Historical / General

1 3 5 7 9 10 8 6 4 2

CIP data for this book is available from the Library of Congress

Blackstone Publishing
31 Mistletoe Rd.
Ashland, OR 97520

www.BlackstonePublishing.com

For all the women gone missing from history

CHRISTMAS EVE

ANNO 1628

New Towne on the James throbbed with merriment as the Lord of Misrule and his mummers paraded through the narrow streets. Their revelry had begun at the fort just before dusk, as the inflamed sun slid beneath the icy veneer of the great river. The villagers had heard the erratic cadence of the drum and the shrill pipes and closed up shop, released the servants, and unleashed the excited children to witness the unbridled gaiety allowed once a year. In defiance of the wilderness that surrounded them, that had on more than one occasion nearly swallowed them, the men in motley greens and yellows, bejeweled with rings and bedecked with bells, danced and sang and romped in the shimmering glow of candlelight. The pagan ritual held sway on this holiest of nights, for in throwing propriety, caution, and sobriety to the winds, the settlers—at least for a few precious hours—could imagine that in their disobedience they were free from the tyranny of man, of nature, and even God.

Temperance Flowerdew understood this and had always

welcomed the annual spectacle, though tonight, from her bed on the second floor, she could see only the darkening sky and the melancholy clouds, swollen with snow that would soon fall like crystallized tears. She eased herself out of her warm bed and lumbered to her escritoire. She ran her hands over the glossy walnut surface, not yet accustomed to the novelty of it. Hardly one to be enamored of fashionable decor, Temperance had first seen the writing desk while visiting the court of King James and knew she must have one like it. Many years passed and none too soon before it was shipped across the Atlantic. Since then, Temperance had made use of it daily, mostly for correspondences, many of which were crammed into the honeycombed recesses of the desk. Tonight, there would be no letters or solicitations or scented notes. She trembled as she reached for the quill. She did not know if she were up to the task, if her courage or her intellect, or both, would fail. A musket blast in the streets and the crowd's cheers startled her. She steadied herself and, with her left hand, dipped the quill—just that day plucked from the right wing of the Christmas goose—into the inkwell.

The story I am about to relate is true. It is not a pretty story; were it so, I should not hesitate to make it known. But these are the facts, ugly and vile as they may be, and cannot, at least not now, become part of the public record. Such an untoward attestation would destroy not only the reputation of my husbands, the first governors of Virginia, George Yeardley, recently deceased, and Francis West; it would also threaten the bone and sinew of Jamestown, a suckling babe in a savage wilderness.

Darcy's familiar staccato rap on the door stopped Temperance cold. She covered the paper with her arm just before Darcy, who never waited for permission to enter, bustled in.

"Checking on the fire, m'lady," she said, reaching the narrow stone hearth in two strides and poking the embers back to life. She hoisted a split pine log onto the dying fire and waited for it to burst into flame. The orange light accentuated the heavy folds and crevices in her face and caught a rare glint of fear in her otherwise unflinching gaze.

"Darcy, I am well enough to do for myself. I have given you permission to go join the celebration. So, go!" She shooed her away with her hand.

"I've seen enough of that foolishness in me lifetime." She rested her small fists on the bony protrusions of her hips. Darcy had come alone from England five years before, a widow, leaving behind five grown children. "It were me that flew the coop," she'd once told Temperance, chuckling. "'Twas the only way I knew to make the silly goslings I raised leave off and grow up."

"Why are ye not abed?" Darcy asked.

Temperance glared at her, which was sufficient reprimand for the old woman to check her tarrying, but not enough to keep her from stomping off. Temperance wet the nib of her quill once more and put it to the coarse gray paper.

Much is already known of our brave little settlement, whose brief history has been amply recorded and, dare I say, amplified by our leaders in various works, not the least of which are those of the honorable John Smith, the most prolific of the lot. Other accounts that have followed—whilst laded with salacious bits fed to English readers ravenous for adventure—are woefully lacking in certain crucial particulars, one of which compels, nay, commands that I take up the pen. In so doing, I am aware that I stand accused of transgressing, for God did not intend for the weaker sex to write. Neither did God, I am fairly sure, (though I am no Puritan) intend for women to sport the corset or the bodice, but these are items which gentlemen seem far more loathe for their ladies to forbear. Write I shall, without permission or apology, not for myself, not even for all women, a presumptuous task that is beyond my ken. I seek only to honor one unsung woman to whom I owe, we all owe, a debt of gratitude, for without her Jamestown might well have gone the way of the Lost Colony.

Those of my generation who find such feminine efforts repugnant will be spared the ignominy, but also the glory, of what I am about to reveal. Once completed, this testament will be locked up and hidden until, God willing, such a day arises in the distant future when it is recovered and the annals of Jamestown history are complete.

"Mama, the snow!" Francis stood outside her closed door.

"It is lovely, Francis," she called back, trying to keep her voice free of impatience. She knew what his next words would be and so spared him the effort. "Yes, my darling, you may enter."

Francis fumbled with the handle and burst into her chamber. She smiled, steeling herself for his rough embrace. But he ran past her to the window. His dark eyes were greedy and his ruddy cheeks stained with the thrills of the Yuletide, the raucous parade, and now the snow.

"It falls from the heavens!" He pointed toward the sky.

"I see you are wearing it."

He eyed the clumps of fresh snow splattered on his wool coat. "I showed Mary how to make a snowball!"

"And throw it, no less."

"Mary's mama says there is no snow where she comes from."

"Africa? I suppose not." She shifted in her seat. "Are Mary's parents dismissed from service early and enjoying the parade?"

"It is a holiday, Mama!"

"Of course." She smiled, watching him brush the snow off his coat. "Your little friend has deft aim."

"I will get her back apace."

"Where are your sister and brother? They're supposed to be watching you."

He shrugged.

"Francis? Where are Argoll and Elizabeth?" She was all too familiar with his chicanery. So like his father, George, she thought. Though how prescient they had been to name their youngest after the man who would become her second husband.

"Argoll is a mummer now!"

"He's gamboling about with that riffraff?" A searing pain shot through her side. She was glad he did not face her.

Francis nodded. "Bessie said I was too little."

"And what is her excuse for allowing you to run loose?"

"Dunno. She was sparking with Harry."

"A Polish taverner's son," she groaned, more to herself than to Francis. "My children, the great levelers. It is a new day in the New World. God help us."

"Ah!" Francis cupped his hands to the window. "Bessie's coming for me." He turned and shot past her out the door. "G'bye, Mama," he shouted, "I shall bring you a bucket of snow!"

She suffered a pang of regret that Francis had not stopped to enfold her in his arms, though, for a brief moment in his wake, it felt as if he had. She stifled the tears that were becoming a daily affair and a nuisance.

I pray God will forgive me for my dissembling, for I seek to disclose but also to withhold. I do not claim courage or fortitude as a motive for recording my story, for it will not in my lifetime, nor those of my children, see light of day. Rather, I am driven only by great urgency. For as much as I wish to ensure the survival of His Majesty's footprint in the New World, and to protect my family, I bear witness in secrecy, but bear it nevertheless, for an entirely different reason. I am soon to die. The child in my belly is most intent, I am certain, on returning to his heavenly Father's loving arms, and will not be content unless I am in tow. My womb is sorely infected, and I have the ague. My husband Francis, with whom I have shared a marriage bed for less than a year, refuses to accept my prognostications. It is no matter. His tender mercies will not alter my affliction, and I must make haste. The truth must be told ere I die with it.

Temperance closed her eyes and searched for the girl's face, lodged in her memory, but indistinct, as if she were viewing her through frosted glass. She begged the Muses for clarity, waited with the patience of Job, then opened her eyes.

Her name was Lily, though I called her Fleur de Lis after the first time she saved my life.

THE THIRD SUPPLY

JULY 1609

The slight, fey maid from Sussex saw what was coming long before anyone else. She had no instruments to aide her in predicting the weather, nor access to the detailed logs of the *Falcon* that would confirm her suspicions. But she knew. The Third Supply to Jamestown, all nine ships and five hundred passengers, was in grievous danger.

She shivered violently on the deck, though the sea air was warm and the sun near midpoint in the clear sky. She tapped her chest rapidly with her fingertips.

"What are you about?" An older woman, a seamstress, perhaps in her late thirties, eyed her suspiciously. "You're not gettin' sick, are you?" She sat on a pile of rags. While she watched the girl, her nimble fingers sewed a button on a cassock.

"No, ma'am," the maid answered, quickly gathering herself. She reached into her pocket and clutched the small crucifix.

"Any more sickness, won't none of us make it to St. James's Day."

"Yes, ma'am." She wanted to blurt out to the woman that in

her premonition she had seen an enormous wave surging toward them. But she was far more afraid of people than she was the forces of nature.

"You the girl what works for Temperance Flowerdew? Lily, is it?" The woman grimaced, as if the scrawny, towheaded lass with eyes as clear as raindrops were an offense to her.

She nodded.

"Then get on with you," she barked. "Make yourself useful, lest I bend your mistress's ear."

Lily hurried away, more in urgency than submission. Temperance Flowerdew might believe her. And though only a few years older, she was a gentlewoman to whom others would listen. The risk to Lily was small. Mistress had been nothing but kind to her during the seven weeks she had been in her service at sea. A friendly easiness had sprung up between them, quick as dandelions. Temperance knew nothing of Lily's past, the reason her mother and father had tearfully given her up to the Jamestown adventure, as a way to start anew. If mistress scoffed at her vision, Lily would seal her lips, not opening herself to the charges that had plagued her in Sussex after foretelling one too many such calamities. Not that it would matter if no one made it out alive.

Lily surveyed the deck crammed with settlers. They were tired, sick, and bored from the long, monotonous journey. London, from where most of them originated, and which itself was filthy, overcrowded, and disease-ridden, seemed Edenic compared to this unsanitary tub on which elbow room was a luxury and death lurked around every corner. But with landfall nigh—Captain Martin had said six or seven days—smiles and laughter permeated the gloom that had for weeks covered the expedition like London fog.

She marveled at their oblivion. They did not possess the second sight that fired vivid images in her brain. Surely, they could at least sense the storm, massive by her estimations, bearing down on them. Even the sheep grazing on the chalk downlands of Sussex's coast knew to seek higher ground days before tidal waves swept whole villages away. Lily wanted to sound the alarm but knew she would be met with derision and likely punishment. Better to whisper a warning to one mindful soul than shout it to an ill-tempered throng. It had been a gift, this uncanny ability, until it became a curse. Her mother had planted her garden by it, which, with its prolific array of herbs and vegetables, became the envy of the village. Her father had consulted with her too, as early as the age of five, before setting out to troll the English channel and beyond for their livelihood. "Yer hair's got the red in it," he'd say, cradling a blond tress. "Ye've seen something." A blizzard or a sun-splashed day, torrential rains or early frost, an impending drought or a gale wind—she recognized them all as she might intimate friends who spoke to her not in words but in sensations.

Lily spotted Temperance cornered by hopeful suitors, as usual—one a boy of sixteen, much too young, the other a man of around thirty-five years, far too old. Lily tried not to run, which might scare off the admirers, though for all that, she already knew Temperance's heart. She approached her mistress with as much calm as she could muster.

"Lily!" Temperance sounded relieved, then quickly changed her tone to a scold. "I've been looking for you." Lily wasn't fooled. Temperance nodded at her suitors by way of dismissal and beckoned Lily to her side.

"You are a godsend," she whispered. "The one brayed like a

donkey with the breath to match, and the poor boy . . . I wasn't certain if he had a bad case of pimples or the pox!"

Any other time Lily might have laughed, and perhaps gently chided her mistress for being too picky, a luxury neither of them could afford if they meant to survive in the new settlement. The storm surged in her brain as if it were already upon them. She leaned in and whispered in Temperance's ear.

"I have seen a thing."

Temperance pulled back and studied her. "Go on."

"It is a gift of second sight," she said nervously.

"What is it you have seen?" she asked without hesitation.

Lily eyed her in surprise. Mistress had taken the news on faith. Lily sighed and described her vision as it had come to her—in a wash of anxiety so strong it had played havoc with her heartbeat, in colors so vivid her eyes had ached, in sound so deafening her head had rung.

"When?" Temperance asked. The color had drained from her face.

"Near midnight."

Temperance stood half a head taller than Lily but never appeared to be looking down at her, as most of the gentlewomen did, even now as she digested the incredible news.

"Are you certain?"

Lily nodded. The two stood stock still as the restless passengers milled around them. The cheerful clamor of voices both rough and smooth, the gentle wind, and warm sunshine belied the looming catastrophe that would soon engulf the flotilla.

"Then we must prepare."

"Will you warn the others?"

"Who would believe me?"

"You are a lady."

"I am a woman."

Lily stared at her. "But if you tell the captain, he might change course . . ."

"The captain will pat my hand and prescribe spiced rum and bed rest."

Lily looked anxiously to the sky. It was absurd, to do nothing and wait for disaster to strike. She wanted to scream. Temperance linked arms with her.

"Heed me, Lily. You will do no good if you blather about doomsday."

"I am not one to hold my tongue when I am foretold," she warned, exasperated.

"It has been your undoing, has it not?"

Lily felt a wave surge within her.

"You knew?"

"It is the very reason I chose you. I had heard of your visions and decided they were a hedge against my bets. And now they have paid off." Her blue-green eyes glittered. "But I need proof."

"Mistress?"

"Your hair."

Lily untied her cap and reluctantly pulled it off her head.

"Blood of Christ! The rumor is true," she cried out. "There are streaks of red where before there were none."

Lily steeled herself for the worst. If the visions weren't enough back home to turn people against her, the sudden and freakish coloration would.

"Does it fade?"

"In a few days."

"I shall expect you," Temperance said, examining a strand as if it were a specimen, "to reproduce this effect for me. Though I should prefer something more subtle. Red does not become me." She waggled a lock of her own black hair.

"Do not jest, mistress." She had expected horror and revulsion, not mirth.

"It's not every day I am met with such novelty," she said, hiding her amusement.

"The hurricane is bearing down on us. Will you do nothing but mock my hair?"

"Surely not," she said, suddenly sober. "I have a plan."

***

At the tender age of twenty-one, I authored my first official document. It was an audacious act borne of a childhood spent in the company of the printed word. I read voraciously in preparation for the voyage, consuming all the maps, books, and pamphlets about the New World that I could gather. With my maps and Lily's help, I was able, in a few short hours, to chart the path of the storm. The extraordinary detail of her vision combined with my rudimentary knowledge of navigation, picked up in the interminable weeks at sea as I nosed about unsuspecting sailors, aided me in crafting a fairly convincing forecast. Using nautical terms liberally like "longitude" and "latitude," "sounding" and "drift," I predicted that if we did not change course, we would surely catch the tail end of the tempest, if not the trunk. I, of course, fabricated large portions; as they are wont to say, Mater artium necessitas. *Enough of it was based on science and metaphysics that I felt certain of my rough measurements. To legitimize it, I signed with a flourish not my own name, but that of a distinguished mariner who had died of calenture only days before.*

He, among the fishes, became the authority by proxy that would keep us alive. Afterward, I laid in wait until the captain vacated his cabin, leaving the door unlocked, and slipped the document into his log. Lily and I had only to watch and pray.

***

By dusk, the ship had not shifted direction. The window of opportunity, which Lily likened to the small portal she peered through, was rapidly closing. Down in the hold, she sat next to Temperance, who, crumpling her shawl to her nose to block the stench of unwashed bodies, was deep into Vespucci's *New World and Four Voyages*. How she could possibly read at a time like this was beyond her.

"Mistress," she whispered, so the other passengers, always elbow to elbow, would not hear. "We stay the course."

Temperance lifted her eyes from the page, taking a moment to shift her attention from the textbook voyage to the real one. She focused on the varied complaints of her fellow passengers, registered in dulcet moans and cynical laughter. She studied them in the dim light, agitated even in repose. The ship echoed their discomfort, creaking and sighing as if all of life were a perpetual lament. She shook herself free of the collective despair, then wet her fingers and snuffed out her candle. Noiselessly, she reached for her cap, the cue for Lily to follow.

On deck, in the open air, they could feel the wind gusting. The sky was bruised with clouds. Fore and aft, the sails of the other ships swelled. The flotilla drifted toward the maw of the leviathan.

"Look!" Lily pointed to the quarterdeck where John Martin was head-to-head with Master Francis Nelson.

"They are in earnest," Temperance said. A strong wind knocked her back. Her white cap flew off her head, leaving her unpinned hair to flap like a tattered black flag on a pirated ship.

The officers, now joined by the lieutenant and the bosun, hastily retreated to the captain's cabin. Within, a single lamp glowed, dancing, as it moved over the various charts, reports, and the counterfeit document she had planted.

"There's an even chance," Temperance said. She explained to Lily that Captain Martin, a quiet and unassuming man, would carefully weigh the evidence, while Master Nelson, narrow-minded and opinionated, would dismiss the report as the delirium of an old man at death's door.

Minutes passed, then a quarter hour. Lily paced, growled at the men's dallying. The ocean swell grew, almost imperceptibly, though not to Lily, who knew the waves gently curling in on themselves, like a sleeping babe's fingers, would soon grow into gigantic claws, pulling them under. "There's still time," she protested. "Why do they tarry?"

Before she could answer, the men sauntered from the cabin looking, for all intents and purposes, as if the most urgent order of business were a game of cards. There was laughter and hearty backslaps before the group dispersed. No orders were given, no alarm sounded. The ship's bow remained steadfastly toward the northeast from whence the storm was gathering.

Lily charged the bosun, crossing the main deck. Temperance made chase and snatched her before she could reach him. He spotted them, just as they had slowed to a stroll, Temperance holding Lily in a vise so tight, there was little she could do but submit.

"Ladies," he bowed. He was short and built like a block of wood. His beard, a flaming red, full, and neatly trimmed, covered half his face. His hard green eyes regarded the women first with surprise, and then, because they were alone in the gloam, with interest.

"The wind, Mr. Bruce," Temperance said, as sweetly as she could, "it is brisk. And the ocean is quite restless."

"Aye, mistress," he said, engrossed more in their pretty faces than chatter about weather conditions. He knew the women on the voyage had been enlisted for a single purpose, to become wives. And though he was not a settler, there was no law stipulating he could not partake of whatever cargo he helped transport.

"Is a storm brewing?" Temperance asked, almost with a simper. Lily looked away, to hide her disgust.

"Aye, mistress. But nothin' to worry yerself about. Captain says it'll blow over in no time."

"Then the captain's a boil brain," Lily bristled. She swiped at the loose hair lashing her face.

"What's that ye say?" he asked, speaking loudly against the increasing noise of the surf and wind.

Temperance pinched Lily's hand.

"We pray that the captain will take every precaution to keep us safe." She forced a bright smile.

"Indeed," the bosun said. "But if yer lookin' for protection, it's me as got the biggest culverin on the ship." He wet his lips.

It took Lily a few beats to glean what mistress already had.

"You forget yourself, sir," Temperance said, taking their leave.

Lily looked over her shoulder at Bruce who, in a parting gesture, cupped his genitals. His impudence gave her one more reason to survive.

***

Lily awoke suspended in midair, assailed by wailing and curses. The ship had listed so sharply to the larboard, she and Temperance dangled on either side of the upright beam they had lashed themselves to below deck. All they could do was watch as the settlers, who had dismissed their earlier entreaties to prepare, slammed into one another. The ship heaved again, to the starboard, slinging the mass of jumbled settlers back across the hold toward them. Lily yanked on Temperance just as an airborne dirk took dead aim. Instead of what surely would have been Temperance's head seconds earlier, the dirk lodged in the oak beam she was tied to.

"We must be alee to the swell," Temperance shouted. "If they don't right the ship, we shall roll."

Above the din of shrieking wind and crashing waves and the howling of the passengers, Lily could hear the men on deck, their muffled shouts and exhortations like those of unmoored ghosts, doomed to haunt the seven seas for eternity. She felt helpless, at the mercy of the ferocious storm, whose next assault she was sure would topple them. She braced herself.

"We're turning!" Temperance reached for Lily's arm. "Do you feel it?"

Lily opened her eyes. The ship rocked and trumpeted like a furious elephant, but it was slowly arcing. The *Falcon*'s bow began to rise and dip, rise and dip. The motion, though only slightly less jarring, was welcome relief, as it meant their ship was now slicing through the enormous waves rather than being buffeted by them.

"Thanks be to God!" A skeletal man, thin as famine, fell to his knees and clasped his hands. He was one of a handful on board suspected of being secret Catholics. In the moment, no one cared. His cry ignited a cacophony of biblical scripture from the settlers, all blessing in one way or another the name that gave and took. A towering swell lifted the nose of the ship nearly vertical to the sea. The settlers slid from bow to stern. For a few terrifying moments, the ship hung suspended in the air before crashing down to sea level.

"How much more of this?" Temperance beseeched Lily.

"My visions don't tell time, mistress." In the turbulent to-and-fro, she felt the panic of confinement. She clawed at the two straps of her makeshift harness, tight around their waists, before Temperance stayed her hand.

"Don't be foolish, Lily. You will be tossed about like flotsam."

Three tars, drenched in salt water and rain, clambered down the stairs carrying lanterns. They spread out along the sides of the hold, their lanterns held high. Quickly and methodically, they examined every square inch for leaks before the next surge.

"Tell us, mate, are we forsaken?" asked a keening woman, who had somehow managed to stay plump after weeks of meager rations.

"Nay, mistress," the oldest of the three, Abraham, responded, not taking his eyes or fingers off the creases in the ship's timber. "She's all a piece."

"Over here!" The second tar, a skittish Scot, shouted. "Stay," he held up a sunburned hand bereft of a ring finger. "It's me eyes. Nothin' but a shadow."

Abraham straightened. "All clear, then?"

Before the sailors could answer, the ship pitched again, sending them staggering as they retreated back to the deck.

"For the love of God. Can you tell us anything?" a sickly man, yellow with jaundice, asked.

Abraham lifted his foot off the first rung of the ladder and turned to face the terrified throng—ashen, bedraggled, unceasingly beset for the majority of the voyage.

"The men are doing their best," he began in a rush, "what with the wind knockin' 'em about like tenpins. The sails are no good to us. Took six stout mates to wrestle the whipstaff and keep us on course. Truth be told, with the rain spilling on us from above and the sea heaving its guts at us from below, we're blind as bats." Lily knew he had wanted to be hopeful, but his own despair had won out. The lantern cast a greenish glow over his gaunt face and hollow eyes. "If only we could get our bearings. 'Tis a muddle. Day is as night, and sea and sky are topsy-turvy. Ye cannot tell the devil from the redeemer."

One woman, clutching her Bible, shrieked. Abraham spun and headed up the ladder without another word.

***

For two days, no one ate and no one slept. The storm battered the ship mercilessly, rendering the besieged settlers nearly catatonic. Only Lily knew when the storm had broken. Just after dawn, as the exhausted settlers drifted off to sleep in spite of themselves, Lily whispered in Temperance's ear. Quiet as falling leaves, they undid the rags and made their way aboveboard. The clouds now covered the sky like tulle rather than a shroud, and the wind blustered.

"Good God." Temperance, her hand to her mouth, surveyed the ship. Everywhere was debris and damage. Sails lying in unwieldy piles, boards torn and splintered, dead fish, some alive, their wordless mouths begging for mercy. A few sailors stood in shock, frozen like ice sculptures at their stations; others were limp, lying face down on the poop deck, slumped against the gunwale, curled in the corner. A lone halberd was lodged, pike-down, through a slumbering sailor's vest, as if he were a giant beetle specimen in an entomologist's collection. In one stroke of luck, all three masts, though denuded, stood unmolested, like the crosses of Calvary.

"We are saved," Temperance said, clutching a piece of rigging.

Lily squinted against the blinding sun emerging from behind the clouds. She searched the horizon in all directions.

"They're gone, mistress."

"They?" Temperance looked out at the vast expanse. "George," she whispered.

Other than the chastened sea, there was nothing to be seen. Not a sail, not a mast, not even wholesale wreckage. It was as if the entire fleet of ships, except for the *Falcon*, had been swallowed whole.

CHRISTMAS

ANNO 1628

It was then, after the storm, that I took to calling her Fleur de Lis. I had hit upon it whilst interviewing her before The Third Supply set sail. She had been the seventh hopeful that day seeking employment as my personal maid, and I was growing quite cross, not having found a suitable match. Mama, finally realizing that nothing, not even taking to bed in a fit of hysteria, could convince me, her only child, to forestall my decision to settle in Jamestown, begrudgingly aided me in selecting a servant. Yet Mama only made matters worse, pointing out all of the flaws of the first six candidates and none of the virtues. She was right, of course, but the last thing any young woman wants to admit is that her mother is right. I was breaking away, after all, from the life she had led, one of relative leisure and privilege, and any reminders of our similarities in temperament or judgment would only weaken my resolve. I was on the verge of another scrape with Mama when—

"Mama, watch!" Francis spun his top on the card table, grazing Temperance's crooked elbow. The table sat in the middle of the drawing room, such that she felt like the hub of the family wheel.

"How clever, dear."

"Watch."

"Once more."

Francis spun it again, so hard it careened clear across the table. Temperance caught it before it flew off the edge and handed it to him. He trotted over to show Argoll, who was fogging the window pane with his breath.

—Lily arrived, as unadorned and proud as the Madonna bloom that bore her name. I heard Mama sniff at her thin frame, which she, but not I, mistook for delicacy. She was young, too, barely sixteen, but somehow old beyond her years. I could see in her squared shoulders and the rash tilt of her head, in those eyes, clear as glass, that she was not to be denied. After the initial niceties, I asked, "And why would you give up hearth and home to embark on an expedition? An especially dangerous one at that." She looked me dead in the eye and replied, "I might ask you the same, mistress." "Impertinent," my mother huffed, whilst I laughed. "What makes you suitable for this position?" I asked. "Have you any schooling?" "Three years, mistress," she said, "afore my family needed me to work." I noted a hint of resentment but I wasn't sure to whom it was directed. "And what are your skills?" Mama interjected. "I will keep your daughter alive," she replied.

"Might I have another cake, Mama?" Argoll asked. The boy ate like a bear fresh from hibernation, though he remained spare and spindly.

"You have had three already. You will turn into a cake."

Francis laughed gaily.

"I don't understand, Mama," Bessie sulked aloud, as if oblivious to all needs and complaints but her own.

"Again?" Temperance sighed. "You regale me with this again? He is—"

"His name is Harry."

"Harry is with family today, as you should be," she said.

Bessie shifted her weight on the divan with great exaggeration away from her mother and toward the blazing fire. Temperance mused that her willful daughter's cold shoulder was quickly and uncomfortably heating up.

"What preoccupies you so? And on Christmas?" Francis asked, wandering in from his own work in the library. He leaned over Temperance's shoulder, his hands clasped behind his back.

"A letter, husband," Temperance said, not bothering to conceal her work, as she knew Francis could not read without his glasses.

"To whom do you write with such urgency?" he asked, almost peevishly.

"Posterity, I hope." She had not meant to say it, as it might raise his suspicions.

"Ah." He frowned, straightened his lean, elegant frame. He stood a moment, expecting the children to engage him. When they did not, he reddened and turned to leave. "Do not tax yourself," he gently admonished Temperance.

I am being taxed, she wanted to say. How she longed to escape to her room to write, but it would not do. The family could have her today, she did not begrudge them that.

Mama snorted, but I knew the girl's strange remark chilled her, as it did me. I asked Lily how she could be so sure, but before she could answer, Kate, my mother's maid, sauntered in with tea. She nearly dropped the tray when she saw Lily. She steadied herself, moved gingerly past Lily, eyeing her as if she possessed horns, and set the tray on the table. It was comical, this rotund tyrant, the only person who held Mama in check, apparently cowed by a country lass. When Kate whispered in Mama's ear, she jolted and cried "Oh!"

"M'lady, the cook has taken ill and begs off. Who shall I have prepare the goose? Guests will be here apace."

Temperance slapped her quill on the table.

"I'm sorry, m'lady. I dunno what to do."

"Speak to the governor."

"I did," Darcy clutched her apron. "He told me to ask you."

"These are *his* guests!" She shoved her paper across the table. All three of her children started as if at a vase shattering. Mama rarely raised her voice.

"I could cook the bird, m'lady," Darcy squirmed, "if raw or burnt be to your liking." She chuckled nervously.

"Who in heaven's name does your cooking?"

"Me Jim." She smiled proudly. "He's a gem." Darcy had rebuffed her second husband, Jamestown's best blacksmith, six times over the course of four years, before she finally agreed to marry him. By then she was nearly fifty, having waited, she'd told Temperance, for her child-bearing years to lift like a midmorning fog.

"Is Jim about?"

"Well, yes, m'lady, if he's not drunk. Christmas and all."

"Fetch him."

Darcy nodded sharply and scampered from the room.

Temperance felt the nausea wash over her. She forced herself to focus on the words.

I fully expected Mama to repeat aloud whatever horrors Kate had related, but instead, she chose to whisper in my ear. "Witch!" is all she could muster, her eyes round as doubloons. Lily rose, seeming wise to the slander. I was about to lose her.

"Enough!" I told Mama. "She will do." I turned to Lily, beseeching her. She smiled, nodded once. And the interview was over.

"Give it back!" Francis snatched at the top Argoll had wrested from him. "Mama, tell him to give it back," he screeched. Argoll responded by dangling it just out of his reach.

"Enough!" Temperance gathered up her materials. "This will not do." And she took her leave.

THE ARRIVAL

AUGUST 1609

The *Falcon* crawled toward Jamestown. The main sail was torn, rendering it useless, but the others were intact, enabling the ship to make slow and steady progress over the three weeks since the storm. Temperance had learned how to measure speed. Pretending to take in fresh air, she would sidle by the navigator as he lowered a board into the ocean throughout the day. The board was attached to a spool of rope that was tied at equal intervals with knots. As the rope unwound, the navigator used a thirty-second hourglass to count the number of knots that passed through his hands into the sea. The more knots, the faster they were moving, which at this point, with limited ability to capture the wind, was not fast at all.

Temperance eyed the horizon, desperate for any sign of the other ships from their fleet, most especially the *Sea Venture*. There, she knew, in the flagship, was housed the new charter, establishing a change in governance at Jamestown. There were the officers and gentlemen who would guide the fledgling settlement, the head of the collective body. And there was the one young man, a lieutenant, who had made her furious enough to throw caution to the winds, disobey her parents, and give up a comfortable home and secure future for an opportunity to prove him wrong.

"A penny for your thoughts, mistress?" Lily joined her on the poop deck.

"Fleur de Lis."

"I told you, mistress, I've done nothing to deserve that."

"The dirk. I should have three eyes and a burial shroud were it not for you," she laughed. "How . . . ?"

"No devilry," she sighed. "I saw the dagger coming straight for you."

Temperance reached for Lily's hand and looked across the sea, tranquil and beatific as a sleeping toddler after a tantrum.

"About the others? Do you have insight?"

"Only the weather. Not people. Is it George you're worried about?"

Temperance turned toward Lily.

"You just said you didn't—"

"For the love of the saints! Don't make my every thought out to be witchery. You talk in your sleep."

"Good God. What do I say?"

"Enough for me to know that you are of two minds." Lily thrust out her palms like scales, weighing air. She laughed and bounded down the steps.

Temperance flushed. Lily had been privy to her innermost thoughts. She could live with that. What set her skin tingling was not knowing them herself.

***

When George had announced his decision to join the Third Supply, Temperance had been crushed. Not because he had wrested her heart, which he had, or even that she was losing a promising suitor, which is what her mother had said. She was crushed because he could so blithely relay such momentous news in an utterly mundane way. They stood together that day on Fleet Street as churchgoers strolled past them. It infuriated her that he spoke about the matter as if it were of no more import than the price of bread. The freedom he enjoyed to go about as he wished was alien to her. She could not enter a library, let alone set sail for America.

"When?" she asked him.

"A fortnight," he said. "I have been commissioned by Sir Thomas Gates of the Virginia Company of London." His round, blue eyes, so guileless, bore into her.

"Are you not thrilled?" she asked, barely disguising her envy.

"Well, yes, of course. It is a great honor. But I should not like to take leave of you." It had been his first admission to her of his intentions. They had known each other for only a few months, and rather than tug at her heartstrings, his longing was the last straw.

"You presume too much!"

George stiffened. He ran his hand over his brown hair, combed and oiled for church, and long enough to curl over his ears.

"I presume only to care about you, to make a name for myself, and return so as to win your hand."

"You, you, you!" she shrieked, not caring what meddlesome Puritan might hear her and report back to her mother. "As if I have nothing to say about it." She stopped, struck by an idea like a blow to the head. "I shan't be here when you get back," she said.

"Oh no?" he asked.

"I intend to go as well." Once she said it, there was no taking it back, not unless she wanted to live the rest of her life choking down her words. She did not know yet what she was after, only that the continent, which beckoned across the sea, held her future, and she its.

George laughed. "You are saucy, but you bluff."

Now it was her turn to laugh. "I heard the Third Supply is short women—respectable women from good homes who will make good wives. I also hear the ratio of men to women in Jamestown is quite in favor of the gentler sex."

George's face drained of color. "You will not last, you will be eaten by wolves, you will be stolen by Indians!" He sputtered. "You will . . . become an Indian!" He threw his cap on the ground.

Temperance laughed again, thinking the last possibility absurd, a clear sign his argument was spent. "Perhaps," she said, "but I will go."

George bowed sharply and left her in the middle of the street. She watched his back, torn, by the headiness of her resolve and a flood of longing for him. She was, as Lily said, of two minds, wanting to stand for herself and with him at the same time. At a loss as to how to reconcile the one with the other, she chose, for better or for worse, herself.

***

Her eyes tired from scanning the sea, Temperance rested her head against the gunwale and tried to breathe in calm. She knew that in her pronouncements to George she had been rash, foolish. Determined as she was to make good on her word, to brave this new world, she was also utterly ill-equipped for it. The skills men possessed to survive in the wilderness had never been any part of her experience. She could not spear a fish, fell a tree, grow food, build a shelter, shoot fowl or game or a hostile intruder if her life depended on it, which it surely would. She didn't even know how to cook or clean properly, that duty given over to servants. What she was good at was reading and mastering dense, arcane, and complex tomes of science, history, mathematics, and politics—much to the amazement of her family and friends, nearly all of whom regarded her skills as amusing parlor fare rather than a suitable vocation for a young woman. The one notable exception was her father, a successful notions merchant, a book lover himself, who had stocked the library for his precocious daughter. When she turned thirteen, he left her without mentor or patron, when he succumbed to an infection brought on by an abscessed tooth.

The memory of her father's winsome face engorged with poison, his gray eyes wide with incredulity and pain, brought on a stinging grief. She covered her face as if to block the image. In its place she pictured herself in his lap, the smell of dye and copper on his hands as he opened a book with the reverence of a monastic. Together they would gaze at the tooled leather, smell the glue in the binding, run their fingers lightly across the brittle paper and florid script. Only then, after their silent ritual, would he, and later she, begin to read. She'd fall fast asleep against his chest, the vibrations from his voice more soothing than being rocked. Later, when she was too big for his lap, she'd read to him. After an exhausting day trading voluminous quantities of buttons, thread, needles, and fabrics, he'd nod off, a contented smile on his face. She'd sensed, as a very young child, that her father had dreamed a different life for himself but had neither the will nor the temperament to pursue it. In the small fortune he had amassed, and with it the books he insisted they read together, he had granted her an unlicensed freedom to flout the boundaries of her birth, not just vicariously through print, but in the helter-skelter of an unfinished world.

In the little time she had before she set sail, Temperance gathered as much information as she could, the best way she knew how, from the books, charts, maps, broadsides, and pamphlets that detailed discovery and exploration. She read about the treachery of a vast ocean with its deep-water currents and sea monsters, of endless trees on an untouched continent, plentiful as porcupine quills, of native peoples, mysterious and beguiling, hostile and welcoming. Among the few possessions she was allowed to take with her on the voyage, she chose a scant two maps and five books, all related to America, which cost a pretty penny and which she studied and read over and over again. While indispensable to her, they were not nearly enough. She had come to the disturbing realization that, rather than having achieved autonomy, she was more dependent on men than ever. And on one man in particular, whom she could trust to have her best interests at heart—if he were not already at the bottom of the sea.

She had met with him once more before they had set sail, when he'd paid an unexpected visit, first placating Temperance's hysterical mother with assurances that he would protect her, and then, in the library, offering her an olive branch. George bowed stiffly and handed Temperance a copy of *Don Quixote*.

"Where did you—?" she began in shock. The gift flooded her with a searing gratitude, which she struggled to quell, as she was not willing to forgive him in an instant.

"A friend of mine, a vintner, procured it while in Madrid."

"I am not fond of the romance," she had said, unkindly.

"It is like no romance you have—anyone has—ever read."

"Do you mean to suggest I am untutored?" She had heard it was blistering satire about a foolish man seduced by tales of adventure, chivalry, and conquest.

He smiled. "You are better read than the mystics."

"Then I am to you as this guileless adventurer, Don Quixote?"

His smile vanished and he set his jaw. "I imply no insult. Can you not accept a gift?" He flushed deeply.

Temperance feared she had irked him beyond repair.

"You are a patron of books. I've given you a book," he said, quietly, controlling his breathing. He turned toward the door.

"Yes. Thank you, George. Thank you," she said. "It is a kindness. Something I am in short supply of."

He stepped back, returning, and fixed his frank blue eyes on her.

"I regret we are not quartered on the same ship," he said.

"Our destination is one and the same, is it not?" She smiled.

He nodded and took her hand lightly in his. "I'll not lie. I've suffered many a sleepless night. I'm still not reconciled." He hesitated, as if fighting a sudden urge to renew his arguments. "I wish you Godspeed." He let her hand slip from his, briefly meeting her fingertips with his own. When he bowed, taking his leave, she noticed that his long hair, the color of seasoned oak, had been newly washed. She reached to touch it, but pulled back.

Time and again during the interminable voyage, Temperance had vowed to tell George, once they reached the New World, how the book had acted on her, this gift, like a footbridge between her father and her suitor. How his thoughtfulness had revealed his core and bolstered her own. But now, she feared the worst, that her fine expressions of gratitude might forever lie fallow. She felt the sickening sensation of loss. The cruelly dispassionate seascape appeared to have swept George away. She felt unmoored, weightless, as if the favorable winds that drove the ship to port might blow her into oblivion. She realized, whether alive or not, he had been her unwitting agonist, the very reason she stood on this ship miles from a wilding shore, the greatest triumph of her life. She would forever be grateful. If she were not able to properly thank him in this life, then such beatitudes would have to be proffered in the next.

A piercing cry of "Land!" from the lookout atop the main mast echoed throughout the ship. As the news spread, the settlers emptied the hold and flooded the deck, pushing past Temperance, craning their necks for a glimpse of terra firma. "There," many pointed to the far distant tree line, unlocking smiles nearly rusted shut after their long ordeal. The sailors slapped one another's backs as if new fathers. Some women collapsed like unhinged marionettes in joy and relief. The faithful, ever the keepers of the Protestant faith, praised God, their sheening faces tilted to the heavens.

Temperance could not believe her ears. Land at last. Her nagging fears gave way to exultation. They had made it. *She* had made it. Others had perished, but she had prevailed. She owed much to Lily, of course, but hiring her had not been simple good fortune; it was a wise decision. Her decision. And she had learned much on the journey about the business of seafaring. She would learn more, by hook or by crook, accomplish that which George Yeardley had insinuated was impossible. She would survive.

***

The *Falcon* anchored at Cape Henry on the Chesapeake. There was much ado as the settlers made preparation to disembark, gathering themselves and their belongings in advance of the pinnace that would ferry them to the fort before day's end. The upper decks resembled a marketplace, stacked with crates, barrels, furniture, trunks. The livestock had to be kept below until the passengers evacuated the ship, but they sensed the impending change, and could be heard—pigs, roosters, chickens, horses—like an orchestra warming up. There was much merriment and goodwill as the long confinement and physical deprivation were soon to be a thing of the past. The din overhead irritated Temperance who, hunkered in a nook in the armory, could not concentrate on Thomas Harriot's account of Virginia, the one book in her meager library upon which she relied the most.

"Aye, mistress, ye plannin' on stayin' here, moonin' over yer poetry?" Mr. Bruce loomed large. He smiled, though it looked unnatural.

"I do not read poetry." She slapped the book shut and rose quickly. When she looked over his shoulder, she saw that they were alone. Having gotten lost in Harriot's description of the native Wiroans, she'd not noticed that the armory had been emptied lock, stock, and barrel.

"What is it that yer readin', then? A romance?"

She clasped the book to her chest. "No. I do not read those either." She forced a smile but averted looking into his flat green eyes. She focused on the sharp lines of his fiery beard. He was so close she could smell his skin, acrid, as if soaked in bile. When she tried to slide around him, he blocked her. She felt her hackles rise. "Let me pass," she said, still not looking at him.

"Not 'til I see what yer readin'." His voice turned hard.

"For what purpose, Mr. Bruce? I suspect you could not read your own name, let alone a book."

He leaned in. "And I suspect," his sour breath warmed her face, "yer a sly bitch. I seen ye. I know 'twas ye who planted that log."

She blanched. No one, she was sure, would believe him.

"You are drunk, Mr. Bruce. Step away."

"Nay, mistress, sober as a pilgrim. Don't touch the stuff. Ye knew about the storm ahead a everyone else. Everyone, that is, except the witch." He backed off, taking pleasure in this lightening strike. "One word from me and she'll be ablaze ere dawn."

"You have no proof."

"Don't need any. Saw it with my own eyes that night we met. Weren't ever there afore, not in all the time I watched her traipse about. Tress a hair red as Satan's tongue. My word is good enough."

"I will deny it."

"Then ye'll fry with her." He laughed. "I suspect," he mimicked her in a high-pitched voice, "ye wouldn't want that."

"What are you after?" she asked.

"A little comfort, is all." He came toward her again and fingered her book. She pulled it away. "I fancy a woman who reads like other mates fancy teats."

She felt cold and nauseous all at once.

"And you'll leave Lily alone?"

"Oh, no. It's the pair of ye I'm after." He snatched the book out of her arms.

"Surely, Mr. Bruce, instead of hands and feet, you possess hooves."

"I'll remember that keen, when I've mounted and yer witch is astride." He clutched the pages of Harriot's report, then ripped them out in chunks, tossing them on the floor at their feet. He flung the cover on top of the pile and left Temperance there, to put what pieces she could back together.

THE WELCOME

AUGUST 1609

The farther they traveled up the James, the heavier the air became. Worse than the West Indies, where the sweltering horse latitudes claimed a few sickly settlers, this heat was dense and wet, like a fever. Even those who didn't sweat except after vigorous activity broke out in minutes, struck by the oddity of their weeping bodies. Escorted on both sides by an eerily quiet army of pine, oak, and sycamore trees, the settlers became so still the only sounds were the mopping of brows and sighs of discomfort.

Lily had savored the voyage, but as they left the ocean behind them, entering into what seemed endless forest, she felt melancholy. The salt air, which she had been tasting for weeks, turned, smelling of mud and freshwater fish as they sailed inland. Instead of ebullient, she was dour. Perhaps it was because she had lived her entire life on the coast and did not relish the prospects of a cloistered peninsula with only a river to recommend it. Even her brief trip to London for the audience with Temperance had made her skin crawl.

She strained her ears in the stillness, hoping to pick up any signs of life. Their arrival seemed like a trespass, all of nature becoming instantly alert and guarded. She felt watched, as if by onlookers at a funeral procession, with a mixture of curiosity and dread. She peered into the forest and caught no movement and no color other than muted browns and a riot of greens. There was something else too, darker, so subterranean she could not put her finger on it, as if what they were about to embark on was less God's work than the devil's.

Mistress, she noticed, had said nothing since boarding. She appeared wan and distracted, her hands nervously tucking strands of black hair into her cap. Lily wondered if the stark reality of Temperance's imagined life had settled in. She was sharp as a knife and resourceful, but she was also a gentlewoman, for whom simply making a bed, let alone taming a wilderness, was a novelty. Lily knew the veneer of civilized life would give way to every man for himself. Most likely it would be food that set them at one another's throats. Already the shortage on board led to pilfering and hoarding. She silently thanked her mother for insisting Lily take the seeds she had harvested from the garden. Lily did not know if they would grow, but as all seeds do once planted, they gave her hope.

As the pinnace followed the bend in the river, the solid wall of trees became checkered with sandy bottom, just enough to sit and fish or dry off after bathing. A blue heron on the banks looked like an English dandy at court, disdainful of the riffraff floating by. A giant mottled turtle on a rotten log basked in the pulsating sun, sliding into the river just as the boat passed. The first sighting of wildlife stirred the settlers, who sat up to gawk.

Just as Master Nelson cried "Jamestown," cannons boomed,

and the resultant puffs of smoke drew all eyes to their new home. Lily felt her heart lurch in her chest. She leapt to her feet. Temperance stood with her, the earlier listlessness evaporating as the fort came into view. Settlers stretched their necks and stood on tiptoe. Anticipation and heady excitement grew. Whatever flights of fancy they had indulged, whatever dreams kept them out of despair, kept them alive, now collided with reality. The utopia they had nursed in their imaginations for months, even years, was little more than a stick-built village on the edge of nowhere. There was no turning back. There was only this.

"John Smith is a blackguard," croaked Miles Torne. He was easily the oldest member of the expedition, nearly fifty-five. "He shall hang for this!" Others murmured agreement, though they had no power or authority to execute him. Nor did they have the justification. Smith had written a scintillating letter, that was all. No one had been forced to make the trek to this backwater swamp. The newcomers had few options other than to replace as best and quickly as they could, one ignis fatuus with another.

As soon as the pinnace weighed anchor, the gates of the fort flew open and men poured out. Shouting "hurrahs," they tried to beat one another to the gangplank. Lily laughed as they pushed and shoved, their arms outstretched to the women, any woman, whose hand they desperately hoped to win, or at least hold ever so briefly. Lily hung back while the men pawed at the few women stepping gingerly on solid ground for the first time in months. In the midst of the swarming pack, one stout yeoman with a profound limp and a small black dog at his side bowed and offered Temperance his arm. She accepted, laughing heartily at the good-natured howls from disappointed suitors.

Lily relished the chaotic merriment, setting aside her earlier foreboding. When she spotted the shy young man at the edge of the crowd, she forgot herself all together.

He had emerged from the fort last, holding a bow and fiddle. The promise of music alone would have caught her attention. But what captivated Lily was his reluctance to look up at what surely must have been a welcome sight. She watched him as he adjusted the strings, settled the fiddle on his shoulder, and leaned his cleft chin gently against the wood grain. He paused, closing his eyes to the sun, which lit up his hair and mustache, wiry and golden. She stood stock-still waiting for him to strike the first note. When it came, she had only a moment to enjoy it before a sailor, not much taller than a dwarf, grabbed her arm and twirled her around. He spun her until, breathless and filled with hilarity, she begged for mercy, nearly toppling into the shallow water. The sailor snatched the belt on her dress, steadying her and begging pardon. When her dizziness passed, she realized that the music had stopped and the young man had vanished.

***

I cannot, to this day, explain the sensations I experienced upon first sight of Jamestown. It was as I had expected, having read those other accounts of the New World, John Smith's notwithstanding. Even so, I took a breath when I saw the crudity in design and construction. Surely, after nearly two and a half years of existence, I thought angrily, the English can do better. I took another breath, filling my lungs with what I realized was the purest oxygen of a pristine forest, the likes of which I had never known, even in the English countryside. On the heels of my dismay rushed feelings so strong I feared a grave imbalance of my bodily humors. With the feelings came a torrent of thoughts, ideas, plans for the future—both mine and Jamestown's. Where others saw deprivation, I envisioned abundance. Where others wilted under the seemingly insurmountable and fearsome task ahead of them, I could not wait to begin. I suppose, in looking back, what I experienced was no mystery at all. It was the elixir of opportunity.

***

On the arm of her lame and loquacious gallant, Temperance listened politely as he regaled her with tales of derring-do, while she assessed the prospects of Jamestown. She knew from her reading and selective eavesdropping that location was vital to the success of any settlement. Choose wrong, and the experiment could meet a swift and disastrous end. Commerce and security went hand in hand. Ease of shipping and natural barriers to hostile natives and foreign threats meant that the settlers would be well stocked, financially viable, and safe. As it was, the fort, Temperance surmised, appeared well positioned. It was a considerable distance from the Chesapeake Bay and Atlantic Ocean and thus tucked away from trolling warships. Sentinels at Jamestown would be able to see the enemy sails from a great distance, which would allow them time to arm themselves. The fort sat on an island surrounded by the James River, save for a slim isthmus connecting it to the mainland, which could easily be secured in the event of an Indian attack. Shaped like a triangle, the fort proper was fitted with a cannon-armed bulwark at each vertex, two facing the James River to the east and west, the third pointing north and inland. Adjacent to the triangulated fort was a slightly larger enclosure, rectangular and less fortified but also secured by palisades.

The river, at this juncture, was an unencumbered route to the ocean, and deep enough for large ships to dock on the bank just north of the fort without having to rely on smaller boats to ferry goods back and forth. But the depth of the river directly in front of the fort was too shallow for the likes of Spanish galleons, eager to square off and blast the settlers into oblivion.

"Did ye hear me, mistress?" Her guide, Cord, held onto her arm. "I was sayin'—"

"Yes, yes." Temperance homed in on his bright, brown eyes, which shone with good will. She could not tell if he were twenty or forty, until she noticed his crow's feet and streaks of gray in his eyebrows. "You were not here a day before you were beset by Indians." She bent down and scratched the head of Cord's little black dog. It growled.

"Spike, mind yer manners." He grabbed the dog's snout until it stopped snarling. "He's a good boy, that one. Just too big for his breeches." He scratched his hindquarters, causing the dog's taut tail to go limp. "Saved me from a snake not two days on land. Copperheads, they call 'em. That big," he spread his hands about four feet apart. "And thick as an oar."

Temperance winced. Cord laughed, picked up the dog. It looked smug in his arms.

"He keeps me alive, he does. I don't go nowhere without him."

"Your bodyguard," Temperance said, noting the dog's alert ears, even as he enjoyed his master's embrace.

Nearing the entrance, Temperance turned the bulk of her attention to the next security feature, the palisades. Built of oak and poplar, the fence appeared sturdy and of a good height, nearly twice as tall as she was. Each log in the fence was spiked to deter intruders from clambering over, at least not without paying for it.

All in all, it afforded some protection, though wood was not stone or brick and could be set ablaze or, with collective force, breached.

Once inside, Temperance felt instantly buoyed. No more than three acres, and quite compact, the settlement was a veritable ant colony. Every corner of it bustled with industry, with officious settlers moving in and out of close to fifty buildings, including a church, barracks, a factory, storehouse, row houses, and a guardhouse. Except for the church, which was brick, the other structures were traditional mud and studs with thatched roofs, so that the fort resembled an English village. Men carried in the supplies from the *Falcon* and would eventually lade it with goods to be sold back in England to compensate investors. Temperance had heard that the hunt for gold had been a wild goose chase and that the settlement had only managed to eke out a profit in timber. But she saw all manner of commerce, the fruits of their labor, from tar and pitch to soap ashes and blue glass for making bottles.

"Is the glass made there?" She pointed south toward the large rectangular factory built into the palisade wall.

"Oh, no. That's where the mooncalfs tried to squeeze gold outta Virginia dirt." Cord rolled his eyes. "They're still sifting through it for other metals, I hear. And a Pole's set up his still there. But mostly the place is used to trade with the Indians. The glasshouse," he threw up his arm inland, "is about a mile off, where there's plentiful sand, and trees for firewood. Though it's no use. The glassmakers, Dutchmen they were, ran off and joined the Indians."

She looked at him.

"'Tis true," he said, reading her. "Not but a while ago. Treason it was. Working for the Indians now. Living like Indians."

"For what possible reason?"

"They were more loyal to their bellies than to England." He

patted his stomach. "It's what comes from allowing a few foreigners in."

She thought back to George's absurd charge that she might succumb to the Indians. It had not occurred to her at the time that hunger could make for odd bedfellows.

"What do you do for food?" Temperance interrupted Cord, who was quickly onto another tale, this one a gruesome account of a settler, who, having committed some indiscretion against the Indians, had been captured, dismembered, and sent back to the fort in pieces.

"Mistress?"

They stood at the entrance of the open-air smithy, inside the rectangular addition to the fort. A blacksmith's anvil rang out and a fire glowed like a setting sun.

"Food. How do you all manage?"

Cord scratched his chin.

"It's a trial. I won't lie. But we got nets and weirs set in the river," he pointed south. "This summer we caught enough sturgeon to feed an army," he chuckled. "Beyond the fence is our garden. Me and about twenty other mates take care a that. And out beyond the garden, we planted a hundred acres of corn. I'm the only real farmer, though. Rest of 'em don't know a hoe from a scratch-back!" He laughed at his wit. "Got livestock, too, foraging nearby in the woods and on Hog Island. What we don't grow or raise, we get from the Indians in trade."

Temperance asked him if the crops and livestock were fenced. "No, no," he said, too casually, it seemed to her. "We keep account." She wondered what in the world made them believe that the Indians would not steal, attack, destroy their food supplies, including the livestock apparently free-ranging for the picking. She had read of Smith's exploits with the Powhatan chief, which had been amicable, and mutually beneficial. But other Indian tribes were not so hospitable. A fence with sentries was hardly provocation; it would be a sensible precaution. She also was surprised that they still relied on Indians for some food. And if Powhatan simply decided to halt trade? Did the leaders of the settlement not suspect Powhatan's motives in providing sustenance? What had continued to set him apart in their esteem from the other natives who had turned on them?

"And water?" she asked, half afraid of the answer.

"Ye got more questions than an owl," Cord laughed. "The drinking water comes from the dug well." He pointed across the commons. "As for the rest, it falls from the sky, just like it does back in England, mistress." He poked her in the arm and winked. "Though, the rain has been a cruel lover since I been here, two years now. Dry as a virgin's—" He checked himself. "Bone dry, mistress, but it shan't last much longer. Drought's about spent."

Confounded again by the management of the settlement's most vital resources, she wondered what would happen if the well ran dry, or the crops shriveled and died. But she was pried loose from Cord by Master Nelson, who reprimanded him with narrowed eyes, then led her away.

"You must be careful, Mistress Flowerdew, that you not mix with the lower sorts." He looked straight ahead as he talked, clutching her arm. Nelson was taller than Temperance by a head. She felt imposed upon by this man whose authority over her had ended at the gangplank. "It will be difficult, I know, in such small quarters, but all the more necessary. For propriety and the sake of social order."

Temperance bristled. Not in the New World a half hour,

and already it reeked of the old. She had felt warmly embraced by the rustic and, she realized, safe from the vicious Bruce. She wanted to expose him but could not say a word, lest she risk endangering Lily.

"Cord was quite helpful," she said. "A perfect gentleman."

"No doubt. But there are rules."

She wanted to shake free of his arm, but he kept a firm grip.

"And who are the law givers?" she asked. "Here, I mean. Who makes those rules?"

Her tone stopped him. He looked down on her for the first time, his lean face and long pointed nose reminding her of a fusty childhood tutor.

"They are natural to the English and unspoken." He guided her into the doorway of the end row house. "You are a gentlewoman and will be much sought after."

"And so, like a prized sow," she said, looking into the darkened interior of the cheerless abode, equipped only with two chairs, a table, and two canvas beds, "I am meant to idle in this pen,"—she swept her arm across the room—"until such time as a gentleman sees fit to breed?"

He chuckled, not sure whether she was joking or in earnest. "Jamestown is desperately in need of a woman's touch." He let go her arm and took his leave. Temperance immediately backed away from the dreary threshold into the sun, shaking off Nelson's shadow. She surveyed the vibrant settlement and again felt the exhilarating rush of possibilities it afforded. Here were unchartered waters. A frail slip of humanity had deigned to start the world anew, free from a body politic that had grown corpulent and fetid. She did not know yet how she would fit in, or make her mark, only that it would indeed include a "woman's touch," whether at the hearth or the altar or the lectern or the market square. For here in this place she could do or be whatever she wanted. It did not matter how they tried to enforce the old ways, the past would not hold, it would not hold.

JOHN SMITH

AUGUST 1609

He was short and hatless, his thick brown hair badly in need of a brush, and his profuse beard like a Devon hedge ripe for clipping. He was still young, just turned thirty, with the bearing and dress of a commoner. But he was John Smith. And there was no mistaking the man who had become a legend. Such men are rare. Their exploits titillate entire nations and entice scores of dreamers to risk everything for the promise of a life fully lived. So it was with Smith, who, disembarking from his sloop, strode through the settlement as if it should have been named after him instead of the king of England.

Temperance watched from the church door as he passed through the square, a vortex attracting men, boys, dogs, and even a gray goose. Devoid of the ruff that marked aristocracy or the breastplate of a soldier, he looked ordinary in his doublet, linen shirt, and breeches. He exuded extraordinary energy in his stride and single-mindedness, hailing those joining his ad hoc entourage and making haste for whatever urgency had pulled him back from his exploits beyond the fort.

Temperance wondered from whence came such self-assurance. Smith had been born to mere farmers and, later, apprenticed to a shopkeeper. Had his father, who kept the restless boy in check, not died when Smith was sixteen, Smith might never have ventured beyond his native lands. As it was, he began his career as a soldier and privateer soon after his father's death, which brought him fame and riches and the opportunity, at the tender age of twenty-seven, to become a ruling member of one of the most ambitious efforts at colonization in Great Britain's history—the Virginia Company.

But Smith's temperament favored exploration over husbandry. Though he had risen to the position of de facto governor of Jamestown, he often left the settlement for long stretches of time—mapping the region, seeking food, negotiating with the Indians—only to return to a village in disrepair, dissolution, and dissent. Temperance had heard that his efforts to impose his will, at the expense of political expediency, had resulted in political mayhem and, worse, two near misses at execution. The man, she mused, tempted fate for sport.

"He is fulla himself, that one." The seamstress, Nancy, stopped outside the church near Temperance to take in Smith, who was fast approaching. She pressed a basket full of clothes to her hip. The bright green of her eyes was amplified by the rosacea that blotched her skin.

"He seems a force of nature," Temperance said, waving away the flies.

"Aye. He can fill a codpiece, all right." Nancy guffawed. "Beg pardon, mistress."

"Ladies!" Smith paused, bowed slightly. "Welcome to our frontier hostelry. You improve it by your presence." Nancy tucked in her double chin, tittered, and curtsied.

"I hope to do more than enliven the scenery," Temperance said. She had not meant to be sharp, but something about this man instantly irked her. Perhaps it was the ease with which he assumed authority, and casually dismissed hers. She felt a burning in her stomach. It had flared at other points in her life, impelling her to rash decisions, not the least of which had landed her in this foreboding coastal tidewater. It was inconvenient now, hardly reasonable or prudent, for she had hoped to emulate this remarkable man, not antagonize him.

Smith took her in from head to toe.

"I am Captain John—"

"Yes. I know."

He shifted his weight. "Then you are at an advantage, for you are a stranger and a woman whose acquaintance I am forbidden to make without permission."

"This is not London, sir. We might have to wait for the Fourth Supply to convey a matron suitable to introduce us." A few of the onlookers nudged one another. "Or, you could do something radical, which I hear is not uncommon for you, and simply ask my name."

Smith let out an incredulous grunt. He eyed her warily, assessing whether she be friend or foe.

"And yet, here *you* are," he said. "One of only a handful of intrepid women. Perhaps you and I are of a mind."

"I'm Nancy, sir," the seamstress blurted out, edging her way between them. "And this is Mistress Flowerdew."

"Flowerdew," he mused. "Such a delicate name for one so formidable. I should have thought—"

"Cold pike?" a freckled boy piped up. Every one of the men laughed.

"You!" Nancy put her basket down and pointed at the boy, who was enjoying the moment. "I'll teach you some manners." When he mimicked her by wagging his finger, Nancy lunged at him. He dodged her and scampered off.

"Nay," Smith said, tugging at his beard, laughing. "'Pine needle' is more what I was thinking."

"And why is that?" Temperance asked, lifting her chin.

"You give me something to chew on."

This time Temperance laughed.

"Well," she said, slowly waiting for the hooting to die down, "that depends on whether or not you actually have something left to chew with."

Smith put his hand to his mouth then quickly withdrew it.

"To be sure, Mistress Flowerdew," Smith said, his face bright red, "my bite is far worse than my bark." Before bowing and walking off, he looked at her the way she had hoped for initially, as someone to be reckoned with.

***

They met again, a week later at the landing, as two more ships of the Third Supply, the *Diamond* and the *Swallow*, lumbered to shore, bringing the total to six—the *Unity*, the *Lion*, and the *Blessing* had, days before, also found their way to Jamestown after somehow surviving the storm. The hope was the last three ships would eventually follow, including the *Sea Venture*, which carried the men chosen to replace Smith as president. She had heard the news of his unwillingness to relinquish power. The captains of the arriving ships insisted that Smith step down, citing the dictates of the Second Charter. Smith argued that because the charter very likely went down with the *Sea Venture*, it was not binding, and that if or until said document materialized, he was still the president.

Smith was right of course, and Temperance wondered why the Virginia Company had not seen fit to make multiple copies of the document, distributed to other ships in the flotilla, in the event of the very conditions that now left them in political disarray. Without the charter, she knew Smith was the person with whom she would need to ally herself, at least for the time being, if she hoped to gain leverage in the settlement. She could not rely on the absent Yeardley. Each day that passed without any news of the flagship dimmed her hopes but strengthened her resolve. She would do this without him, perhaps in many ways because of him. She determined to forge her own alliances. That meant Smith. If he were in her corner, she could negate threats, the most immediate of which was a redheaded officer with a penchant for blackmail. But given their icy introduction, during which she surely lost ground, she now had to opt for a different tact. And she needed help.

"I'm to do what, mistress?" Lily asked. She had come to the landing at Temperance's behest, though Temperance knew her maid had more pressing matters to tend to, like finish unpacking, clean the bedding, which was infected with lice, haul the ash left in the hearth, set up her meager kitchen supplies, and till the soil for their garden. Lily was also eager to have a look at the livestock grazing outside the fort, which she hoped included sheep for wool and milk.

"I must have his ear," Temperance said, trying not to stare openly at Smith who was surrounded by his usual coterie of sycophants.

"Why is that so important, mistress? We need to set our household in order."

"I've no skills in that regard. I have ideas."

Lily stifled a laugh. Temperance knew well enough that ideas were a luxury in this rude Zion where survival meant backbreaking work and relentless vigilance, where comfort was not a silk pillow or upholstered cushion, but a sprig of lavender from the garden to freshen the inside air or a handful of rue to chase off the fleas.

"Well, I've an idea," Lily said pointedly.

Temperance turned sharply to her.

"You leave the captain to his duties, and you and I—"

"What? Clean, cook, fetch, shoo, churn, hoe, mend?"

"That's about the half of it."

"I'd rather read," she said, realizing too late how ridiculous and self-indulgent it sounded. But her evasiveness was not entirely unintentional. She needed as yet to keep Lily in the dark.

"So would I. But my mum put a stop to that. And a good thing it was," Lily said, unconvincingly. "It's the business of staying alive we must tend to."

"I would be dead in under a year if that were all I was about."

"You'll be dead if you don't."

Temperance shrugged.

"You must learn how to feed yourself, mistress," Lily pressed.

"I've no appetite for such pursuits," she said dryly.

"Wit does not fill the stomach," Lily said.

"I've taken stock," she snapped. She did not wish to hear her own nagging concerns about food aired in this moment. "The settlement is well-provided."

"For how long?" Lily asked. "Look at them," she tilted her

head at the new arrivals filing off the boats. "Hunger presses against them."

Temperance did not need to look at them. She herself was hungry. It was a new and frightening reality. Her solution, though, veered sharply from Lily's. Rather than become proficient in the particulars of self-sufficiency, for which she had no aptitude, she opted to inveigle her way into Jamestown governance. She had no experience, except secondhand, through her exhaustive reading on such matters. She was as eager to enact her municipal plans as Lily was her domestic ones. Lily, she surmised, could procure a king's ransom for the two of them, but it would make little difference if Jamestown collapsed in mayhem.

"Now!" Temperance saw her chance and gave Lily a little push. "He is alone. Make haste!"

Lily scurried toward Smith. Halfway there, a young man Temperance recognized as the fiddler came directly at Lily, his head down. Lily spotted him and stopped. If the fiddler did not look up, he would run right into her. Temperance tensed, not sure what possessed Lily. There was Smith, about to be accosted by two fawning women fresh off the boat, and Lily was suddenly frozen in place. The fiddler lifted his eyes and caught Lily's. He slowed, as if coming up on a patch of ice, then raised his arm in an awkward greeting, and held it there. The women were nearly upon Smith. Lily hesitated a moment longer, then abruptly left the stricken fiddler and angled toward Smith, cutting off the women and delivering her mistress's message. Her duty done, she spun around, looking, Temperance realized, for the fiddler, long gone.

In watching it all, Temperance felt every bit the ringmaster in a bearbaiting contest. Lily had gathered herself and beat out the two women, and many others, conveying what she hoped would provoke the ursine Smith into lumbering over to her. It worked. Temperance took a sudden interest in a group of boys playing fox and goose.

"Mistress Flowerdew," Smith said to her back.

"Captain Smith." She waited a beat, then turned to face him. She met his eyes.

"You employ your maid as envoy. It is not customary."

"No. But effective, I see."

He took a breath and pulled in his lips.

"The maid—"

"Her name is Lily."

"Lily is quite the dissembler. She says only that you favor my ear, which you may be able to prevent from being cut off."

"She repeats what I have told her, nothing else."

"I am not ill bred, mistress, but my patience thins. What do you mean by this?"

She knew it was time to play her card. Another few seconds and he would be gone, having dismissed her for good.

"Captain Martin and Master Nelson are desirous that you relinquish your presidency."

"That is common knowledge, given the manner in which gossip spreads here like the yellow fever." A soldier, putting a horn to his lips, blasted out a signal, which Smith paid heed to like a hunting dog. He bowed and turned.

"I have the means to forestall their attempts to depose you."

Smith swung back to her.

"There is a document on the *Falcon*, an entry in the captain's log," she spoke quickly, "that foretold the storm in great detail and accuracy. The entry was ignored, and the results, as we all know, were devastating."

"So," Smith's eyes flashed, "Martin and certainly Nelson knew about it and did—"

"Nothing. They did nothing."

"They could have changed course, alerted the other ships," Smith fumed. "How in hound's hell did you know about it?"

"That is my secret."

"Do you suspect the document is still there?"

"That is for you to find out. Martin and Nelson will be far less eager to strip you of office if they know you have in your possession such damning evidence of their incompetence. Imagine the wrath here amongst the settlers and sailors. Much of the food that was to keep them until spring most likely lies at the bottom of the sea. And imagine the reception abroad, with the investors, Prince Henry and the king himself. Three ships disappeared, along with the human cargo critical to the success of the settlement."

Smith nodded, tugged at his unkempt beard.

"And why are you so eager for this to be in my possession?" he asked.

"You are best fitted to govern Jamestown."

He raised an eyebrow.

"Jamestown still stands," she said, anticipating his skepticism.

He nodded, acknowledging, though not prideful of, the simple fact.

"And," she added, coyly, "I hope you will be grateful."

He laughed. "Now it appears I am beholden to two maidens. Have you been in league with Pocahontas?"

"No, but you have given me food for thought."

"Then I am doomed."

They laughed together for the first time.

"How might I express my gratitude?" he asked, struggling to read her intent.

"I suppose, when I have something to offer, that you'll lend me your ear." She longed to be more specific, to regale him with plans for Jamestown, but knew it was neither the time nor the place.

"I would consider it an honor." He smiled quizzically. "Well," he said, "it appears I have a mission to attend to."

"Captain Smith," Temperance added, as casually as she could. "Besides Martin and Nelson, there was one other person who knew about the log. A redheaded fellow."

"That would be the bosun," he said. "A Mr. Bruce."

"So it is."

***

Whether John Smith ever made use of the fictitious log was uncertain. A day after the Diamond *and the* Swallow *docked, Mr. Bruce was taken quite ill and confined to the ship. I confess to savoring the news of his particular ailment, a fit of dysentery, which was to my mind incontrovertible evidence of God's perfect wisdom. I prayed that delusion might accompany his needful purgation, thereby calling into question any accusations he might hurl at Lily. As for Smith, he had a mark on his head. When the members of the council and the newly arrived captains of the Third Supply continued to press for his resignation, he appointed Captain Martin as his replacement. Poor Martin lasted all of two hours. After shouldering the weighty burden of the settlement, he gladly handed the presidency back to Smith.*

In the middle of their political backgammon, the newcomers, sorely malnourished, were desperate for fresh food. The bulk of provisions that was to bolster the Jamestown stores sat in the hull of the

Sea Venture. *Any hopes of its survival, or the 150 souls on board, one of which was my George, while not entirely dashed, grew darker by the day. Arriving empty-handed did not suffer the passengers to forebear. Instead, they stripped bare, like a plague of locusts, an entire field of corn. It had been meant to feed the settlement for the winter, but now, it was gone. Lily managed to gather a share of it, but that was little comfort.*

In full recognition of the dire situation, Captain Smith made haste to dispatch the most able-bodied men to disparate posts along the James River in order to gain what sustenance they could from the Indians. We watched as the men amassed in the marketplace dour, grumbling, and unkempt. It was a marvel to witness Smith extol the virtues of the expedition, as if he were Moses exhorting his chosen ones to the Promised Land rather than a military leader possibly sending men to a gruesome death. His enthusiasm, while far short of infectious, did have its desired effect, as the men straightened their backs and set their caps. Smith's officers appeared equally resolute, though I detected in them a seething resentment that in his fervor Smith seemed oblivious to. After his remarks the group made its way to the entrance of the fort and then promptly, as if on silent command, split in two, one group led by my second husband, Master Francis West, which headed north to the falls, the other under the command of Master George Percy and Captain Martin, bound for parts south, to engage the Nansemond Indians. Their departure left me feeling oddly grievous, as one does after a gathering when family and friends take leave. Here we were newly arrived, and already we had been rent. I was incredulous. Instead of plans for expansion, discovery, greatness, we were, the lot of us, caught up in a most unforgivable predicament. Of all that was required for survival, we lacked the most essential. We needed food.

***

Wahunsonacock, *mamanatowick* of the Powhatan Chiefdom, stood outside the gates of the fort. Rather than announce his arrival, which he considered undignified for a great chief, he and his men waited beneath the midday sun. The English had spotted them just as their canoes floated into view upriver. There was a flurry of activity in the bulwarks that made the Powhatan men laugh. Wahunsonacock knew the lookouts had sounded the alarm and that they would gird their loins. But after all the bluster and posturing, the sentries would admit them, even though they were no longer on friendly terms. The English could not afford to send them away because their survival depended on it. This day, Wahunsonacock bore no conciliatory gifts or generous offerings of venison. He had indulged them for a while, but it was time they were weaned. Their incessant demands for food had taxed him, exceeding any benefits he had gained in keeping them alive. He had learned all he cared to about their weapons, and the glass beads—once a novelty—were hardly a fair trade for the corn growing increasingly scarce. Now, their feckless behavior had made matters worse. The hogs the English had let loose to forage were pillaging their fields. Wahunsonacock would have had them slaughtered to compensate for their losses, but the weather was too warm. The meat would spoil quickly before it could be salted or consumed. He opted instead for one last act of diplomacy, out of the compassion his mother had raised him to always embody, and out of his respect for the man he had regretfully plotted against but failed to kill—John Smith.

When the gates opened, Wahunsonacock cursed. His

brother, Opechancanough, touched his shoulder and pointed to the horde of settlers crammed into the little outpost.

"They have increased tenfold," Opechancanough said. "The strangers grow stronger. And there are women and children." He had wanted to wipe out the first wave of Jamestown settlers two years earlier, to put an end to any future attempts at colonizing in their chiefdom. But Wahunsonacock, as the older brother, held sway, overruling what he considered a rash and unnecessary measure. He was convinced at the time that the mutual benefits of cultural exchange far outweighed the threat of a handful of ill-equipped Englishmen, most of whom would eventually die, leaving the dispirited survivors to pull up stakes and slink back to England. He wondered now if he had made a terrible mistake. The women and children were a shock. It meant only one thing—that the fort dared to grow roots.

"No, brother," he said, gathering himself. "They are far weaker. The little ones will be a burden. More mouths to feed. Which now," he said, trying to make light, "hang open at the sight of us." He spoke softly as they made their way past the curious onlookers. "If they do not die from starvation, they will surely catch flies, and so deplete a common enemy."

Opechancanough did not laugh. He kept a keen eye on the settlers, whom he did not trust. Wahunsonacock shared his brother's disdain. The settlers, those who had been at Jamestown fort the longest, regarded the Indians warily or kept on with their work, barely taking notice, especially since the Powhatans came empty-handed. It was the new Tassantasses, true strangers, who gawked at their naked torsos and the blue paint on their faces. He heard one woman whisper about his hair, long and braided on the left side of his head, shaved on the right so that it would not go

tangled when he discharged an arrow. A little girl stood stock-still at the sight of them, then screamed in delight and ran. He wanted to throw their sneers and mocking laughter back at them, draped as they were from head to toe in all manner of costume, the likes of which the Powhatan reserved only for special ceremonies. The women in their caps and hoopskirts looked like quail skittering about, while the men, with their beards and bulky vests, resembled bears standing upright.

Opechancanough smiled as he likely saw in a flash the animal shapes his brother had silently conjured. They looked at each other briefly, to acknowledge the shared vision. Their laughing eyes, the color of pine bark, and mirror images of each other, said, in effect, "Yes, I see it too." It was a gift, this simpatico, but also a burden. Wahunsonacock was so intimate with his brother's spirit, he could not always distinguish himself from this other and often struggled to reach sound conclusions to vexing problems. Opechancanough did not enjoy the same degree of insight into his brother's spirit and suffered no such confusion about his own opinions, especially in regard to the English. In the last two years, it had become the blade that was cleaving them apart.

"Ah, the peacock," Opechancanough said aloud. John Smith approached with several armed men. Wahunsonacock knew his brother did not understand why he cared so much for this dangerous interloper. He had saved him with food on numerous occasions, had taken him in and feted him as an honored guest, even had inducted him into the tribe in a ceremony that included his favorite daughter, Matoaka, whom Smith deigned to call Pocahontas. Smith had been terrified of the tribal ritual, certain he was about to be executed but spared in the nick of time by the young girl. Lost on him was the symbolic nature of the ritual, which

dramatized his death as an Englishman and subsequent rebirth as a Powhatan. There would be many more misunderstandings, until not just Opechancanough, but also Wahunsonacock realized the breach between the cultures was too vast for peaceful cohabitation. The first blow had been Wahunsonacock's earlier attempts to have Smith murdered. In spite of his treachery, the mutual affection and admiration between the two men somehow persisted.

When Smith greeted them with a nod, Opechancanough returned a stony stare.

"You will hunt today, Chief Powhatan?" Smith asked, testing the waters.

Wahunsonacock could see his brother cringe, as he always did, at the misnomer. Wahunsonacock *led* the confederacy; he was not named for it.

"Yes, we will hunt today, Captain English," Opechancanough responded.

Wahunsonacock laughed, shaking his head at Smith's confusion.

"I pray that I am not the trophy you seek," Smith said, without a hint of humor.

"Not today, no," Opechancanough said. "But there is always tomorrow."

The Powhatan chief laughed again.

"My little brother is in a mood. Your hogs have been eating our corn."

Smith put his hand on the sheath in his belt. Opechancanough clutched an arrow in his quiver.

"The hogs do not know the difference between English and Powhatan corn," Smith said. "Perhaps you should erect a fence to keep them out."

"Now that they carry our corn in their bellies, we would more likely welcome them in, to increase our store," Wahunsonacock said.

Smith reddened, pulled in his lips so that the hair of his mustache and that of his beard, met. Wahunsonacock knew the man's temper.

"We shall make every effort to contain our livestock henceforth." Smith kept his hand on his sheath but relaxed his grip on the weapon. After all, the Powhatan outnumbered them just beyond the gates.

"What about the corn that the hogs have already stolen?" Opechancanough asked.

"There is little we can do about that," Smith said, losing patience. "Unless perhaps you are inclined to eat hog shit."

Wahunsonacock laughed, slapped his seething brother's back, but there was no real mirth in it. This experiment with the English had come to a head. Starvation loomed. He had seen its devastation in his lifetime. He felt an intense flood of grief for his friend, John Smith, who was a man after his own heart. Wahunsonacock knew his brother did not understand his attachment to this brash Englishman because he did not know what it meant to be a great chief. Smith was one of the very few men he had ever known to assume the crushing burdens of a nation and a people whose fate rested in his hands. On first meeting, they had both recognized that their actions would determine the course of human events. They had said as much to each other, on many a night amidst the smoky entrails of a campfire, over a pipe, savoring the delectable rewards of the hunt or the harvest. It was both humbling and empowering, for they were mere human beings, wielding the scepter of gods.

The two leaders also knew that one of them was doomed. This certainty in no way lessened Wahunsonacock's respect or affection for the Englishman. It did, though, intensify his ardor to defeat him. Smith's arrival was the harbinger of things to come, that life as he had lived it in the coastal plains of the nation called Powhatan, would soon cease to exist. But he clung to the hope that the English or the French or the Spanish could be absorbed into his world view. Signaling to the men that surrounded him, he took one last look at John Smith, and held his hand up in farewell.

DROUGHT

SEPTEMBER 1609

Lily had set her basket of corn in the corner of their row house, rather than outside, where she feared it would be stolen. As was her habit each night before bed, she studied it, a mixture of worry and concentration on her face. The garden she had put in could not grow fast enough. She calculated to the day when she might harvest the first edible leaves or flavor their bland food with savory herbs. Next to her at the roughly hewn table they shared, Temperance, a book open in front of her, scratched notes, stopping occasionally to hold up the paper to the candlelight.

"Your vigilance will not increase our fold," Temperance joked. They had supped on corn cakes about the size of their palms and washed them down with English ale. She tried not to think about the long hours before their next meal.

"Once the leaves turn, mistress, I can gather acorns and mix them in with the meal. That will fortify it."

"We will not have to subsist on a peck of corn. There are other stores," Temperance said, peering into her inkwell.

"The sailors are hoarding what's left on the ships, or sellin' it to the Indians."

"Is that so?" Temperance finished her sentence and blew on the ink.

"And," Lily raised her voice, "the men laze about and do not hunt or fish."

"Many are ill," Temperance said, gathering her papers together, "or malnourished."

"That never kept my father from a net or a weir," Lily retorted, miffed by mistress's nonchalance. "He worked harder and longer when food was scarce."

Temperance cradled the book, which she had borrowed from Rev. Robert Hunt's collection. She lovingly gazed at the gilded black cover and smelled its sweet pages, already deteriorating in the heat and humidity. Lily recalled how Temperance had cried out when they discovered the small library in the church, unattended and gathering dust nearly a year after Hunt's death. Reading was apparently a luxury nobody but her mistress could afford. Temperance was especially taken with the English translation of Montaigne's *Essays*, and had done little else but pore through it, saving for last his chapter on cannibals, which, she assured Lily, would aide her in understanding the Indians.

"The fall garden's in, mistress, but it may be for naught." Lily stood up to stoke the embers of the fire, which even on a warm night could not be allowed to go out. A cold hearth meant the laborious task of striking flint against steel to ignite a spark, setting it to tinder, nursing the tiny flame with her breath, and hoping the kindling would catch. She wanted to teach mistress the skill of fire-making, but for now there were more pressing matters. "Some of the herbs should be hearty, but the vegetables will be at risk."

"I have all the faith in you, Lily," Temperance answered absentmindedly, admiring again the front matter of the book.

"It's not faith I need," she said sharply. "It's water."

Temperance put her book down.

"You've had another vision," she said.

Lily nodded, pulled a strand of red hair from underneath her cap. She looked directly at Temperance, worry like a caul on her face, her eyes glassy. There was silence save for the drone of a few mosquitoes. Temperance waited.

"Is it the drought?" Temperance asked. "Cord is certain that it has nearly run its course."

"He is not keen," Lily flared. "The drought lingers . . . and will for years."

"You have seen it, in your mind?"

Lily shook her head, her pale skin drained of color. "I feel it." She tapped her chest.

"Perhaps the Indians will teach us how to survive," Temperance spoke quietly. "They are quite resourceful."

"No one lives without water."

"They are still here," she mused. "There is that."

***

Lily went on to describe her sensations in disturbing detail. Suffocating heat that made her skin feel as if it might crack and peel, a desperate need to slake her thirst lest she turn to dust. It was as if she were the very soil, rendered barren and unable to bear fruit, unable to sustain life. Famine would be the end of days, signs of which already swirled around, but which in my sunny optimism and unrelenting ambition I refused to acknowledge. When Lily finished, I petitioned God to have mercy on us. I looked from her to the book on the table, which just moments before had given me such joy. It now appeared a lumpish and stupid thing, filled with the fooleries of vainglorious man. It could not keep me alive, could not, in the throes of all-consuming starvation, offer even comfort. And yet, in that moment, it was all I had.

***

The Indian girl was slightly shorter and a few years younger than the others in her group, but it was clear, by her freedom to consider a stranger openly, she was the leader. She wore a deerskin skirt, a leather strap across her shoulders, and a shell necklace. Her hair was shaved on both sides of her head, and a braid ran the length of her back. She had dark, quick eyes in a handsome face. Her skin was tawny and smooth. All of this Lily noticed only after she had overcome the shock of the bare-chested Powhatan announcing herself as Pocahontas.

They met headlong in the forest beyond the fort. Lily had gone to forage for berries, nuts, seeds, herbs—anything she could gather that could be used for food. When she came face to face with the troupe, her first instinct was to cut and run. But, except for a few mushrooms she could not safely identify, her basket was empty. And so she opted for what Temperance had called diplomacy, which she interpreted as the fine art of securing what she needed without getting killed. The risk was not great, as she had already heard tales of the princess's good deeds and saw their chance meeting as a sign.

"No good," Pocahontas, whom Lily guessed was roughly her age, said in a hoarse voice. She pointed to the mushrooms, crossed her arms over her stomach and playacted heaving.

"It will give me the puke?" Lily asked.

The girl turned to her friends and shrugged her shoulders. They shook their heads.

"The puke," Lily repeated, then imitated the girl's actions, adding with a flourish the wracking sound one makes getting sick.

"Yes, yes!" She nodded, then delivered her own guttural noise, deeper and more prolonged. The others quickly joined in, setting their belongings down and bending over in mock anguish. Lily thought they sounded like a herd of startled sheep. When she laughed, they all joined in.

The girl stepped toward Lily and ran her hands down her thin arms.

"You are hungry."

"Yes." Lily looked into her eyes, which flashed a mixture of concern and shrewdness. She picked the mushrooms out of Lily's basket and threw them on the ground. "Here." She pulled Lily toward the base of a tree where a speck of yellow poked through the leaves. She reached down and gently uprooted a mushroom as delicate as an iris. "Cook," she made a stirring motion with her arm, then held her other hand up to her mouth, "Eat." She guided her to other kinds of mushrooms nearby, all easy to identify for the transplanted Virginian, one that was black and wrinkled, and another that had a solid black core when split open. Lily proved a quick study and snatched at the mushrooms with a fury that made her acquaintance laugh anew. When her basket was full, she curtsied to the leader. The leader pulled her close and whispered to her, the other girls at a distance but watchful. Lily, rapt, responded with a series of questions which the Indian carefully answered. When they had finished, the leader stepped back and with the others, still keeping a sharp eye on Lily, melted into the forest.

***

The smell of the frying mushrooms made Temperance's mouth water. Lily sautéed half of what she had gathered in a skillet over the fireplace embers. She had been careful to separate the mushrooms, hiding the potent ones Pocahontas had been so secretive about until she could find some use for them.

One egg of unknown origin sat on the table. Lily had spotted it on her way back to the fort in an abandoned nest beneath a giant longleaf pine. It had not smelled rank, so she put it in her basket along with the mushrooms, pleased she had secured the evening meal in less than an hour.

"How much longer, Lily?"

"Soon, mistress." She turned the mushrooms in the last of the lard allotted her. When they had softened and were bubbling, she reached for the egg and gently cracked it on the edge of the skillet. Inside was a fetus, its bulbous head blue and its curled body skeletal. Repulsed, Lily tossed it in the fire. It went up in a burst of garish purple and yellow flame. Lily quickly realized she had been rash. They should have eaten it.

***

Lily hauled the buckets of water, one in each hand, from the river and made her way back into the fort. It was her fourth trip that morning and still it would not sate her fledgling garden, scorched by the late summer heat and the unremitting absence of rain. She could have given up, as had so many of the other settlers, but if there were a chance she could eke out a few fresh greens, herbs, and vegetables, she felt it well worth the effort. She had wanted to plant corn, which she could harvest right up until the first frost in November, but there wasn't room in their small plot. Instead, she had planted smart, sowing the beans first, which grew fast, followed by the herbs. Her mother had taught her herbs were not just the staple of a well-stocked kitchen, but also powerful medicines. Parsley enlivened food and doubled as an emetic. Lavender not only perfumed the air but relieved stress and aided deep sleep. Fennel soothed the stomach. Her favorite, rue, was something of a joke between her and her mother. Besides its use as an insect repellent, the pungent plant was said to cure a variety of ailments—from earaches and headaches to poor vision and croup. It could also induce vomiting in the event of accidental poisoning. But what made it special was its two most notorious attributes, the ability to ward off witches and to ignite second sight. "See there, Lily," her mother, who scoffed at superstition, had teased Lily after her first prediction. "It's the rue, isn't it?" When Lily was first accused of witchcraft, her incensed mother, to taunt the wagging tongues that condemned her daughter, and to prove her innocence, grew rue in profusion. It was the first clutch of seeds she had dried for Lily's life in the New World. Lily was not surprised when it had sprung up so quickly in her little garden, its green shoots a symbol of hope and her mother's enduring love. All the more reason, she thought, to keep them alive at any cost.

She passed the well near the center of the fort, angry that she could not draw from it and thus cut her trips in half. But the well, the only source of clean water, was running dry, and thus was strictly reserved for drinking. She could hear her mistress's scathing denouncement of such stupidity. "There should be multiple wells," she'd said. "Not one! Here we are surrounded by water and we're parched." Temperance had offered to tote the water with Lily, but, after allowing nearly half of it to slosh out of the pail on her first trip, Lily gently relieved her of duty.

She set the buckets down briefly to catch her breath and ease her aching shoulders and back. She cursed the unblinking sun, already warming the morning, and wondered how much longer until it rained.

"Such a muckspout for one so fair."

Lily looked up to see a figure silhouetted against the sun. She shielded her eyes with her hand and squinted. It was the hermit fiddler.

"You pop up like bramble," she said, smarting from his remark. "If I close my eyes and open them, I'm thinking you will disappear again."

"So, you been noticing me?" He moved out of the sun and stood where she could see him. The fiddler pulled at her heart with his gaunt frame. His voice alone, soft, and friendly, threw her off balance. She had a sudden and intense desire to touch him, a perfect stranger.

"I notice everything. It is how I will stay alive."

He laughed, scratched the day's growth, like flecks of gold, on his chin.

"Shouldn't you be off somewhere playing your fiddle?"

She stood and reached for the buckets. He beat her to it. When she tried to wrest the handles from his grip, they came inches from each other's faces. His amber eyes, rimmed in dark circles, challenged her. She flushed and felt her arms give. When she let loose of the buckets, the relief was so great, she rested her forehead lightly against his chest. He lifted her chin and kissed her. The shock of it sent her off and running.

Lily stayed in the woods for several hours, filling the pockets of her apron with acorns and mushrooms, as much as she could hold, and then some. For the first time since setting foot in Jamestown, she did not feel hunger, only the lasting effects of a first kiss. The unrelentingly harsh life she had suffered since landing sloughed off. In its place was a warmth and comfort. She could have kept kissing him, and satisfied herself with the fresh memory of it. She had been bold, to allow such a thing in broad daylight. Her mother would be apoplectic. But she didn't care. Those taboos were far away now. Here, the rain would not fall, the crops would not grow, but human touch was abundant. She need not be starved. Through it, her body had responded in pleasure, a sensation rare in the daily grind of hard labor and scant nourishment. It might be the very thing that kept her, kept all of them, alive.

If only she could face him. The thought of it sent the blood rushing to her face again. The afternoon grew long, and she knew she had to return soon, or mistress would worry. She steeled herself and made the trek back to the house. There, outside the door, sat the two buckets, still filled with water. In both floated a white marsh lily. She lifted one, gently shook the water off, and slid it between the strands of her hair. Just as she did, the music started, the aching sweetness of the bow stroking the fiddle as it groaned in pleasure, as it released itself in song.

***

News of the disasters assailed us. I trembled at each dire report, which stung like the wretched black flies that hounded us. First, Francis West's men, north at the falls, were attacked by Indians and their number cut in half. Then, George Percy and Captain Martin's men to the south met a similar fate at the hands of the Nansemonds, who were in no mood to barter with those who had nothing to give. When John Smith, at the behest of Percy, sent reinforcements south, they discovered a grisly and fearsome scene. The mouths of the slain English were stuffed with bread, as if to say, "You want it? Here it is."

But worse news was yet to come, since its import could mean the collapse of the settlement. John Smith had decided to venture north to the falls, to ascertain the losses in men and supplies. Upon his return downriver, he suffered a strange and mysterious accident. Whilst he was sleeping in the sloop, the gunpowder on his belt mysteriously blew up. The explosion ripped out half of his thigh, a gaping wound for which there was no medicine or physic. I suspected a failed assassination attempt, but by whom I could not ascertain. He was brought back to Jamestown and, insult being added to injury, placed under guard, accused of dereliction. He would be shipped back to England under the auspices of proper treatment, and to face charges, a grievous, long journey he might well not survive.

John Smith had many enemies, which had kept us in a state of intrigue and mistrust. But, for all of his foibles, he had held the settlement together under the most impossible and unforeseen circumstances. Other attempts at colonization had failed; this one had survived for over two years. Without Smith, in the hands of the untested Percy, there was little hope it would endure another winter.

THE TRANSITIONING

OCTOBER 1609

Temperance stepped out of Mistress Adams's stuffy hut, where the gentlewoman was recovering nicely from the ague, able to sit up and take some broth. Temperance breathed in the cool night air, relishing the break in the heat that had dogged and afflicted them for two months. It brought hope, a lightening of the mood, from the multitude of trouble.

The earth, though, remained as dry as bones. It made for a spectacular display of autumn foliage, the changing leaves like dowagers in one last hurrah, dyeing their faded and brittle hair in a riot of vainglorious colors. Temperance was able to feast daily, if not on food, then at least on beauty. The dwindling supplies in the storehouse meant severe rationing, though Lily's skills at foraging, and the few beans and greens she reaped from the garden, kept them more comfortable than most. But winter was around the corner, and John Smith, whom she had not seen since his accident, was set to sail in a few days. She struggled to push these thoughts away, intent on enjoying a friend's recovery and an invigorating stroll home.

As she made her way past the well, she heard heavy footsteps behind her. It was late; all save the sentries were asleep, their modest homes darkened. She peered behind her, but with little moonlight and no lantern, she saw nothing but pitch. When the footsteps got closer, she quickened her pace, fearing now that an Indian may have breached the walls. She had nearly reached her doorstep when a rough hand covered her mouth. She tried to scream, but her air was cut off. As she clawed and kicked, the man hissed in her ear. She recognized the bosun's thick brogue in an instant.

"Hush, now, and I'll let ye loose. Yeah? Yeah?" He held her tight and close; she felt his beard on her cheek. She nodded quickly. A half dozen different escape plans rushed through her head. He took his hand away from her mouth but kept a grip on her arm. She trembled so that her teeth chattered. "Well look at you, the little mouse. Not the brave one now, are ye?" Temperance said nothing. "Yer a schemin' bitch alright. Got that arsworm Smith to do yer dirty work, snoopin' around. What'd you put out fer that?" He slipped his hand around her neck and flashed a knife.

"He's got the log. You will be ruined," she said.

"Nae, nae," he whispered almost sweetly, his mouth nearly touching hers. "The log's at the bottom of the river, I saw to that. I'm back to me old self, and John Smith is a dead man." He flicked his tongue against her lips and dug his long thick nails into the nape of her neck. She cried out in pain. He shook her into silence.

"Please, leave me be."

"Oh, I'm not going to bother you, mistress, if that what yer thinkin'."

Temperance wished she could see his features, read his intent. He was nothing but a sinister shape.

"Never had to force a woman in me life." With his fingertips, he caressed the nail marks he left on her neck. "You'll be comin' to me. That is, if you don't want to starve. The fort's so low on food, you'll be eating dirt by January. And me ship is sailing in a week. Won't be another supply until spring. Ye'll all be dead by then, won't ye?"

Every nerve ending in her body rankled at his voice.

"I got enough stashed away to carry you and your witch through the winter."

"I come to you where? When?" she asked, scrambling to piece it all together. He was right about the threat of starvation. Her maidenhood in the face of that seemed a small price to pay, especially when he could force himself on her for nothing at all.

"Tomorrow at dusk, beyond the fort near the stand of sycamores. You and the witch. Every day after that until I'm gone."

"Why give us food?"

"Then the crime would be yers, not mine." He let her go and sheathed his knife. She heard him let out a deep sigh. "And it's far better, when yer on yer knees, beggin'."

"What assurance do I have that you will give us the food?"

"Each night I will bring ye a portion of the total."

"There is a condition, which if not met will be the undoing."

"Yer not in any position to bargain," he said, wary.

"I would rather starve to death than sacrifice my servant girl. She is to be left out of this."

They stood in silence. Even the owls were quiet, as if adjudicating the sordid negotiations.

"Half a loaf is better than none," she said, wincing at the analogy.

Bruce spit on his hand and held it out to her. She turned away and ran the short distance to her home, stopping to dry heave. She trembled uncontrollably in the chill air, eventually calming herself so that her ever-perceptive maid would not suspect she had just bargained with Lucifer.

***

Lily sat up in bed, startled by a sharp cry. She snatched the meat cleaver and crouched low behind the door. She listened to the voices bartering flesh, then realized whose they were. The terms of agreement left her numb. When Lily heard Temperance at the door, she quickly backed away, sliding the cleaver under her pillow and easing into bed. As mistress stood over her, she feigned sleep. Lily lay completely still while Temperance paced and sighed through the night. It was a struggle not to soothe her, but Lily knew it was best to let the thing be, to keep silent vigil with her mistress until daybreak, so as not to show her hand.

At dawn, with her mistress finally in a fitful sleep, Lily carefully spread the mushrooms she had gathered on the table in front of her. She separated them out, into neat piles. She wrapped one pile in cloth and placed it in her apron. These she would take to Bruce. The others she chopped and added to the shredded mustard greens, so that when Temperance awoke, all she need do was heat them in the skillet for her breakfast. That done, she gathered a large corn cake and a jack of ale, which she packed in a small basket. She glanced around the room to make sure everything was in order, then headed out the door. Her hands trembled, but she was resolute.

Near the gates she heard his voice.

"And who might this be, brightening my morn?" the fiddler asked. He smiled warmly, his eyes hinting at the familiarity the kiss had wrought.

"Lily." Not knowing what else to say, she asked his name.

"James Owen," he said. "I've waited for this moment. We're properly introduced." He bowed deeply. "Where are you going on such a fine day?"

She felt her resolve melt like iron in a forge. She could not trust her emotions from one minute to the next. It would be so easy to tell him about Bruce, to include him in her scheme, or plan an entirely different one together. But Bruce could ruin it with one word: *witch*. The fiddler would not only reject her outright, he most likely would strike up his fiddle as she was lashed to the stake. She could not risk his confidence.

"I've an itch for some soap. I'm hopin' to trade with the sailors."

"What is it that you will trade?" He looked to see what she was carrying.

"It's a secret." She smiled, hoping to throw him off.

"I'll go with you," he said. "It's not proper for you to go alone."

"Proper?" she asked sharply. Her ardor for him shriveled.

He flushed, shifted his feet.

"You are an unmarried woman in the company of roughs. It is unseemly. Besides, they will drive a hard bargain. I'll see to it they not cheat you."

Lily laughed. If he only knew what she and her mistress had already endured.

"I do not need your help," she said, then added, "Nor do I want it."

The fiddler's face fell. She had wounded him.

"You are proud. I see that." He backed away, staring her down, then turned and left.

Lily took a few deep breaths. Her first impulse was to run after him, fearful that she had cut her chances. She took a step in his direction, then felt the overwhelming grip of fury. He had not fully understood what she was up against, what danger and humiliation she faced in meeting with Bruce. The fact that she had not confided in him was no excuse. His offer to escort her was no comfort, either. A man could not protect a woman all hours of the day and night. What, she fumed, did decent men think happened to women in those seams, when they were at the mercy of far more than being shorted in a trade?

She stormed out of the gates, upriver to the gangplank leading to the ship. The morning fog, thick and heavy in the cool fall air, hung about, like a sheer curtain. The ship's crew was slowly easing into the morning, the men's voices low and gruff as they begrudgingly took to their various tasks. Pipe smoke and the fumes of skillet-fried fish wafted toward her. Once on board, she approached an old tar, his hair the color and texture of milkweed plume, his blue eyes rheumy.

"Where might Mr. Bruce be?" she asked.

"Aye?"

"The bosun. Mr. Bruce," she shouted.

The tar pointed toward the quarterdeck. There, through the fog, she made out the heavyset Bruce, his hands locked on the gunwale, his back to her. She felt the fear rumble through her. In that moment she was a little girl again, Lily from Sussex, whose mother carefully and slowly braided her hair while imagining aloud a grand wedding, someday, for her daughter. Lily's special gifts had put an end to that, but not her mother's oversized dreams. "Just think," she had said to Lily on the eve of the voyage, "you will be a great lady in a new world!" They said goodbye, knowing they were never to see each other again. Lily drew on the memory, of her mother's faith in her, and marched up the steps to Bruce.

"You," he said, first catching sight of her over his shoulder and then twisting around to see if anyone were in earshot. "What are ye about?" he asked, agitated. No doubt, he read her unexpected appearance as clear threat. As she had hoped, he was rattled that she would confront him openly, even at the risk of being called out as a witch.

"You have made a bargain with my mistress. I wish that you bargain with me."

He laughed, relaxed against the gunwale. It must have appeared as if one of his tricks was about to turn on the other. He seemed to enjoy this immensely.

"You've nothing left to trade that I don't already have rights to," he said, playing along. "So, get on with ye."

"I've something better."

She pulled the mushrooms out of her apron pocket and unwrapped them. He snorted.

"Yer one muddled wench if ye think I'd rather eat that," he leaned in close, looked left and right, "than this." He groped her between the legs.

Lily stumbled backward. She struggled to regain her composure.

"Trust me. They are better," she postured, trusting her instincts. "They have special properties."

"So does a Cumberland sausage, but you'll find this more to yer likin'." He reached through the buttoned gap in his breeches.

Lily stared back at him, at a loss for words.

"Well, well," he chuckled, recognizing the confusion in her face. "Yer a virgin. 'Tis as I thought. All the better."

She tried to gather her wits in the face of his perverse desires. She had some notions about sex, having witnessed sheep engaged in amorous pursuit and dogs rutting in the streets. Often, she had heard her parents making love at night, thinking she was asleep. Once, in the middle of the day, she surprised them. But Bruce's lust was something else altogether, and seemed tied to his appetite. Her plan was no less compromised, and could actually be fortified, by her newfound knowledge.

"The taste is not what it's about," she said, forcing a knowing smile. "It is," she lowered her voice, "an opiate."

"Yer lyin'," Bruce huffed, though he took her hand with the mushrooms in it and pulled it close. "Opium?" He narrowed his eyes.

"Better. Stronger."

"I bet they're poison. Yer tryin' to poison me, aren't ye?"

She tilted her head, indicating his fears were nonsense.

"Eat it then," he said, picking up a mushroom and holding it to her mouth.

She had expected this.

"If I do that, I won't have my wits about me to teach you how to find them."

"Eh? And how do you know?"

"Pocahontas." The chief's daughter had revealed to her in secret that day in the forest the powers of the mysterious fungi. "I am likely the first and only stranger in the New World able to identify it. Imagine if you are the second."

Bruce scratched his beard, his small green eyes trained on Lily. She pressed her case, explaining that dried and stored, the mushrooms would transport well in huge quantities. He could corner the market with an unending supply ripe for the picking, that he alone controlled. "Show me," he said.

"There are conditions," she said, keeping her voice steady, though she knew she had him.

"Aye. You wenches and yer conditions."

"Tell Mistress Flowerdew that you've changed your mind. Give no reasons. For my part, I will teach you how to find, properly pick, and grow these mushrooms."

"Grow, ye say?"

"Yes." She was lying, but she wagered it would close the deal.

"And what do you get out of this?"

She looked him full in the face. Her eyes were steady, transparent.

"I want every oat you were to give mistress."

He swiveled away from her, shaking his head.

"Yer a piece a work. Might be more fun fer me to just poke ye." He made an obscene gesture with his middle finger, which she had no trouble understanding.

"Yes, you could do that," she said. "But then you'd have sullied a witch."

Bruce grunted.

"Never had me a witch afore, I'll say that."

When she stared back at him, he looked down, away, studied the air.

"We're wastin' time," he finally said, angrily. "I want those mushrooms. They better be there," he brushed her chin with his fist, "or yer a dead one."

***

Nearly at a run, Lily led Bruce deep into the forest. The sailor was not used to the pace or the tangled undergrowth of the wilderness, and before long Lily could hear him behind her panting and cursing. When they neared a large pond, still capped in a fine morning mist, she stopped.

"There," she said, pointing to a cluster of beige mushrooms growing on a fallen tree at the edge of the pond. They looked like rows of clamshells wedged in wood.

Bruce, bent over double to catch his breath, straightened and squinted. He lunged toward the rotting log and broke off two mushrooms. He put them to his nose and carried them back to Lily.

"Eat it," he said, holding the smaller of the two out to her.

"No. The drug is powerful. I'll be too addled to forage." She chose her words carefully. Lily did not know for sure what effect the mushrooms would have. Pocahontas had only said they induced visions. "We'll gather as much as we can. Tomorrow, we'll come back for more, and every day until your ship sails."

"Eat it, or I'll shove it down yer craw." He pulled out his knife and held it to her throat.

She put the mushroom in her mouth, chewed and swallowed. He grabbed her cheeks with his hand and forced her mouth open.

"Stick out yer tongue," he growled. When she did, he pushed her to the ground, and stood over her. He crossed his arms, muscled as drumsticks, and studied her. After a quarter of an hour, with Lily not writhing or dead, he seemed satisfied. He fingered the other mushroom harvested from the log, then ate it.

"You're a fool." She realized she had not thought this through. She had expected him to force her to demonstrate the effects of the drug. She did not think he would be so stupid as to follow suit. "We'll be senseless before long. We've got to go back."

"I'm not lifting a foot 'til I know this is not a cheat."

"We need our wits if we're to stay out here," she said. "It's dangerous."

"Yer still standin'. And ye got a clear head about ye. So, I'm guessin' a little bit a mushroom won't knock me down."

"I warned you."

He cut his eyes away from her, hesitated a moment, and began cramming his satchel with as many of the mushrooms as he could find. He darted like a child hunting eggs for Easter.

"Fill yer basket," Bruce shouted. "Hurry it up."

She jumped at his command and surveyed the landscape, searching for them. After a short while, her basket was nearly filled. She spied another downed tree crusted with the mushrooms. It appeared to split in two, and then turn into a rainbow of color. The drug, as Pocahontas had warned would happen, had reached her brain. Quickly, she opened her basket and pulled out the corn cake, which she had laced liberally with rue. As she chewed, she silently prayed the herb would live up to its reputation and act fast.

She fought, but soon surrendered to, the burgeoning bliss that crept over her. She spotted Bruce cross-legged on the ground near the pond, laughing, engulfed in a golden aura. He seemed no more menacing now than an innocent boy. She was amazed at the beauty of his red hair and beard, like flames licking the air. He saw her and grinned, pushing himself to his feet, and walking toward her at a tilt. When he threw his arms out, she welcomed his embrace. It was as if they were twins in a womb.

They fell to the ground entwined, laughing. Something deep inside of Lily whispered that this was not good. But she pushed the voice away, relishing the warmth and love that surrounded her. She and Bruce separated and lay on their backs watching the unbroken blue sky that seemed to absorb their very being. They gasped at the formation of geese flying south and lifted their faces to the cool October breeze. Lily closed her eyes and saw her old Sussex home in vivid colors, like sunlight refracted in clouds.

A crushing pressure forced Lily to open her eyes. Bruce was on top of her. She saw in his dazed expression that the drug still held him, but the brotherly love they had enjoyed had taken a turn. He had her pinned down and was hiking up her skirt. She wore no underclothes and felt his feverish hand on her bare skin. She sensed in his fumbling, and the sheer heaviness of his body, that he was disoriented. While he groped her, she felt an overwhelming nausea. Her mouth went dry and sour just before she threw up the contents of her stomach. The force of it hit Bruce like a bucket of water. He fell backward, howling in disgust. She rolled to her knees, still purging, which gave Bruce time to catch her ankle, and drag her toward him. She kicked and leapt to her feet. The movement made her light-headed and dizzy. If she ran, she might faint, and he would be on her. She looked in all directions for an escape route, then, in desperation, dove into the pond. Bruce stormed in after her, upright, his arms held out for balance. She marveled at her good fortune. The sailor was too unsteady to swim. Bruce pushed ahead, hurling foul epithets and fighting the weight of the water. She swam to the middle of the pond until her feet did not touch bottom. She could have warned him, but she doubted it would have done any good. As she treaded the deep water, she saw the surprise on his face when he reached the steep drop-off and plunged beneath the surface of the pond. He resurfaced once, twice—each time swallowing water, flailing, begging. If she tried to save him, both of them would go under, as he in his panic would take her down with him. She decided instead to do the only reasonable thing she could. She decided to save herself.

***

When news arrived that they found Mr. Bruce floating in the pond, I fell to my knees and thanked God. I know it was sinful to relish the scoundrel's death, but if it pleased God to put him out of his misery, I felt it only fitting as a faithful servant to acknowledge His wisdom with humility and, shortly thereafter, a dram of spiced rum. I longed to tell Lily of our near miss with the ill-fated bosun. But something told me I needn't bother. Her wet clothes drying on the line the night before Bruce was discovered, and her bout with the sniffles and a cough, were proof enough that perhaps it was not God I should be toasting.

There was other good news as well. The Virginia, *one of two missing pinnaces in the Third Supply, had made its way back to Jamestown, bringing to seven the number of ships that had survived the hurricane. That left only the* Catch, *the other pinnace, and the* Sea Venture. *My spirits flared like a sulfur match. If the* Virginia, *the smallest ship of the lot, could somehow survive, surely the flagship would not be far behind. I immediately thought of George, and how much I had to tell him, once he arrived. The sensation was so great, I commenced to speak aloud, as if he were in the very room with me. That is how I took to conversing with George Yeardley. Not the flesh and blood man I had known ever so briefly, and who might still have perished at sea, but this imagined one. Careful, lest Lily might overhear and declare me possessed, I spoke with him in private. Our conversations were naturally one-sided at first, given George's noticeable absence. Eventually, I summoned his voice—firm, practical, caring. In speaking for him, I was able to speak with him. I had managed to conjure from nothing a familiar so that, the Fates willing, when George might finally arrive, it would feel as though he had been with me all along.*

***

Temperance heard the gentle rap at her door. There, bent over and gasping for air, was Cord. Spike lay on the ground next to him, panting from the mad dash. She greeted him wide-eyed and fully dressed, already a step ahead of her courier. Behind her was Lily, at the ready.

"He summons you," Cord said, his words whistling through the gaps in his teeth. "Make haste, mistress. The ship sails at dawn."

She nodded, and beckoned silently to Lily, who gathered the freshly laundered rags, and carefully placed the vial in her pocket. Temperance reached for the lantern.

"Nay, mistress," Cord whispered. "No light. 'Tis a secret meeting. None can know about it."

Temperance nodded again and quietly closed the door behind her.

"I'd lief go with you, mistress—"

"No," she said. "I have Lily, and the path is well-worn." She took his callused hand. "I am grateful, sir."

He looked away, embarrassed by her solicitude, and watched them slip through the gates.

Outside the fort and halfway to the ship, Temperance stopped short and listened to rustling in the underbrush.

"Have we been followed?" she asked Lily.

"Nay, mistress." The whites of Lily's eyes gleamed in the moonless night.

"Are you sure?" Temperance looked in all directions, nervously tucking strands of hair that were not loose.

"Of course I'm not sure."

"Lily?" she asked, trying to read her face in the dark.

"Beg pardon, mistress. This new life is pillar to post. I'm weary."

"It's a trial." She rubbed Lily's arm. "I can go it alone."

"Nay, you can't." She sighed.

They hurried on, the cold damp air turning their breath into white mist and frosting the foliage beneath their feet. When they reached the gangplank, it was slippery with moss and rime. They held on to the rope railing and sidled their way to the deck. A boy, sleepy-eyed and cross, greeted them with his lamp and led them to the cabin, unlocking the door. Temperance pressed a coin in his hand. Inside, John Smith lay on his bunk. When they entered, the smell nearly knocked her back. She glanced at Lily who, arranging her rags on a small table, seemed not to notice the stench of infection and rotting flesh. She fought the unbearable urge to cover her nose.

"I did not expect that you would come at the nick," Smith said. He sat up, his back against the partition of his small quarters. His hair and beard were more snarled than usual, and he wore a nightshirt soaked with sweat that was gathered at his hips. "There is risk."

"I am fairly certain you did not expect we would come at all," Temperance smiled. She tried not to look at his injured leg, bare except for a yellowed bandage, and gray as a limb that had been severed.

"Your note, from the valiant Cord, brags of a cure," he said. "I could not refuse, given the alternative."

Lily, without asking permission, began to unwrap the old bandage. As it came off, revealing the bright red of the ragged muscle, and beneath it, the sinew and bone, Temperance swooned. Lily caught her by the elbow. "Look away, mistress," she said, impatiently, "I do not want two nurslings on my hands."

"It is not my cure," Temperance said to Smith, bracing herself. "It belongs to Monsieur Pare."

"Yes, so you said." Smith winced as Lily pried off part of the bandage that stuck to his skin. Temperance stiffened at the skepticism in his voice. It was the second time in as many days she had heard it, the first coming from Lily.

Temperance had handed her the list of ingredients the morning before and asked if she could secure them. She had heard John Smith went untreated and remembered a volume her father had bought her from Pare's *Les Oeuvres*, which was devoted to the proper treatment of gunshot wounds. It had fascinated her, though she doubted that she would ever need to put such specialized knowledge to use.

"Pouring boiled oil over the wound is what you do," Lily had said. "To sear it shut."

"Pare says boiled oil is primitive and dangerous."

"And you're saying, or this Pare is saying, egg yolk, rose oil, and turpentine will do the trick?"

Temperance heard the snigger in her maid's voice.

"You laugh?"

"Nay, mistress." Lily tried to sober up. "I just think instead of dressing a wound with that potion, I'm better off polishing a table."

Temperance had whirled on her heels and stormed out of their home. It took a prolonged walk and growing hunger for her to return. She had wished, as Lily's superior, to admonish her. But the thought of reprimand seemed foolish. She knew her authority ended at the dinner table, where she would be at a loss without Lily as to how to feed herself. And, Lily had become not just her most trusted friend and confidante, but kin. Titles such as mistress and maid seemed arbitrary and capricious in this strange and treacherous world. Temperance had treated her as an equal from the start, or at least she thought. She had quelled her anger and slunk home, grateful that Lily had not foregone her usual ministrations of cooking supper. Together, in silence, they ate gruel and fall greens. Afterward, Lily uncorked a vial she had sitting on the table and waved it under Temperance's nose. When she flinched, Lily laughed.

"It's the turpentine, mistress. That was the easy part," she said. "The men harvest more of that from the pine trees than food. There's no rose oil to be found, so I substituted oil of lavender. The eggs were a trial. I poked around the sandy side of the shore and found a clutch of turtle eggs. It's the best I could do."

"You're a wonder, Lily," Temperance had said. "You could have eaten those eggs, you know."

"I wanted to, I'll not lie," she smiled. "But I thought about you never coming back, and me being the reason, what with hurting your pride, and I realized there are worse ways to starve."

In the dim light of the cabin, Temperance watched as Lily dressed John Smith's wound with the salve. He clutched the edges of his bunk, anticipating pain, but instead groaned in relief. Lily replaced the dirty bandage with a clean rag and tied the end in a neat knot. She patted the captain's leg, set the vial on the table, and stepped away.

"You have the hands of an angel," he said, his head back and eyes closed. "Marry me."

Lily blushed and dipped her head.

"The fever has taken your senses, Captain Smith," Temperance said. "If she marries anyone, it will be me."

They all laughed.

"So, young lady. You have two proposals before you. Whom do you choose?" Smith asked, enjoying the tease. He clamped his hands behind his head and regarded her brazenly.

"Neither," she grinned. "I'm holding out for Prince Henry."

Smith guffawed.

"So you should," he said. "Young Harry would get the better of it."

Lily curtsied with an exaggerated flourish and left them alone.

"I am grateful for the medicine," he said. "My leg, I feel certain, will keep over the long voyage."

"You will be sorely missed," Temperance said.

"I have no choice." He shifted his weight.

"I have heard the charges are—"

"Nonsense. They are the poisoned darts of pygmy."

"You will prevail, I am certain."

"By God's grace, or at least the English."

"I fear for the life of Jamestown."

"It means so much to you," he said. "Why?"

"You need to ask? I can see your leave-taking is more grievous to you than that wound. I turn the question back on you. Why?"

He rubbed his knuckles and gazed at them.

"It is free of other men's imagination," he said. "No. It is free of their *dearth* of imagination."

She nodded, hanging on his words, this uncommon man she might never see again.

"The fort is as yet a half-formed thought, you see." His face contorted as pain shot through his leg. He waited, until it passed. "It has yet to take on immutable shape."

"But you have spent so much of your time away from the fort, exploring. And when you return," she laughed, "you are quite the tyrant."

"Because nature is pure genius. It does not impose itself on itself." He shook his head. "I play the philosopher now, a role for which I am ill-equipped."

"Your wisdom is rough but true."

"After my furloughs in the wilderness, I am dismayed. Each time, the fort, though it grows in size, becomes more rigid and narrow."

"The old world imposes itself upon the new," she said.

"Yes! I see it, and I can't help but behave like the whale's blowhole!"

"It is your way," she laughed.

"It has gotten me here."

She studied him, frail and dispirited as he languished on his sickbed. It occurred to her that his storied career as adventurer, explorer, and founder, was over.

"My reasons for choosing Jamestown were somewhat less lofty." She wanted to tell him about George, and the part he played, but decided such intimacies were best kept private. "I had a temper tantrum."

"Ah!" He laughed heartily. "We both suffer short wicks."

"So it is that your own gunpowder exploded?" She had meant to be quick-witted, not leading. It had a sobering effect.

"'Tis fitting."

"Though suspicious."

"I am the enemy of the near-sighted," he said, putting an

end to her speculation. "What keeps you here? You could sail with me this day."

The thought had occurred to her. To be free of hunger and disease and privation, to lay to rest her ambitions and the vanishing hope of George's return, filled her with enormous relief. But something even more powerful kept her wedded to the dismal outpost. The unbroken and unclaimed landscape and the fluid boundaries of the settlement's social order—threatened by, but still resistant to, English custom—gave rise to a way of life forbidden to subjects of the Crown. Jamestown could not remain English if it were to survive. It needed the Indians and their survival skills, the Dutchmen who once crafted the glass, and the secret Catholics who whispered illicit prayers to their crosses. It needed men of all stripes and backgrounds. It needed women. And because so few were willing to leave their comfortable homes, it afforded the ones who did an unprecedented freedom to do and say as they pleased. She could not, would not now, relinquish such heady authority.

"I am bewitched by possibility," she said, almost coquettishly.

"Ha! Then I hope you will finish what I started."

"I?" she asked, incredulous. "How?" She realized he was passing the mantle, of sorts, to her.

"Diplomacy is the art of the weaker sex."

"I am quick to anger."

"You will learn if you hope to have a hand in reshaping from within this triangulated eyesore."

"You dream large, Captain Smith."

"It is the only kind worth having." He stretched his hand toward her. "Now, help me into my clothes. I am to be displayed on board as we depart. It will not do to bid farewell in my drawers."

***

At the break of dawn, the largest surviving ship of the Third Supply flotilla drifted past the fort. As if observing a floating funeral pyre, the settlers had gathered on the banks of the James, solemn and downcast. They shivered in the cold and grieved, at the loss of both their last major transport out of Jamestown and the leader who had kept them alive. Smith gamely stood on the deck, wane and grim, lifting his hand in salute to the place which he had founded and to which they feared he would never return.

The brisk chill of the late October air was yet another cause for bereavement. Fall was dearly departed; winter loomed. The food supply was chronically short, the Indians had turned their backs on the settlers, and there was no hope of resupply until spring. As the ship reached the bend in the river and then sailed out of view, the settlers silently trudged back into the fort. Loss was not only something they would endure but inevitably become.

THE SIEGE

NOVEMBER 1609

George Percy fingered the fine tablecloth he had been given by his mother, the countess of Northumberland. "A bit of civilization amongst the barbarians," she had said, and which he repeated to his dinner guests. He told them how he had gratefully accepted the white linen edged in lace—and packed it with his bone china, silverware, and crystal—as a hedge against the insurgency of the savage, to which he was neither suited nor attracted. It was on full display this day outside of the governor's house on the long cherry table that had been set up in the commons. Percy sat at the head of table, dressed in a crisp ruff, gold-lamé doublet, and royal blue silk breeches. His long narrow face and hands were pale and soft, a clear indication that, unlike John Smith, he was not an outdoorsman. Even dining in the noon sun seemed to tax him.

Temperance sat next to the new president, stunned at this affront of a lavish meal in the midst of deprivation, but too hungry to stand on principle and boycott it. She had been one of the invited guests, considered by Percy enough of a gentlewoman to earn a seat amongst the Jamestown elite. To ease her conscience, she wore a skirt with deep pockets, in which she would secret as many scraps as she could to take home and share with Lily.

When Percy was finished delivering a truncated prayer, he raised his hand to the steward, an officious middle-aged man with a bald spot at the crown of his head. "I will deliver remarks forthwith," he smiled tightly. "Let us first refresh ourselves." Temperance could see the collective relief that the food would not be delayed.

She said little through the first few courses, a pale consommé which had not been properly defatted, and raw oysters from the James, tasting more of the river than the delectable saltiness of the ocean. She quietly observed the ten other dinner guests and Percy. She was only one of two women, the other, Jane Blythe, the fiancée of a gentleman named Bacon. All of them except Percy seemed a bit sheepish at such extravagance. She noticed they kept their eyes on one another or their plates, as if ashamed to look at the men and women in the commons who could see the ample fare but not partake of it.

Percy sipped his soup and sucked his oysters loudly, then delicately wiped his fingers on the linen napkins that the gossips claimed he had laundered and pressed daily. His brown eyes, large but not wise, darted greedily around the table for more. But even at the president's table, portions were limited. While waiting for the next course, Percy interlaced his fingers, as if constraining his appetite, rested them on the edge of the table, and addressed his guests.

“I am pleased you could join me,” he said dryly.

The diners laughed heartily, the whetted edge of their hunger blunted temporarily by the seafood and broth.

“The next course, I promise, will quiet your complaining stomachs.”

“Will it work on wives?” asked Bacon. He had a sallow, pockmarked face that seemed perpetually aggrieved. The diners laughed at his sarcasm, and then harder when his fiancée huffed, arms akimbo, in mock offense.

“And what about the rest of the winter?” a gentleman named Worth asked sharply. He was young, with a bulbous nose, blond goatee, and thick red lips. The guests dropped their smiles and cut their eyes to one another and Percy.

He shivered slightly, though the weather was mild, and seemed to struggle to catch his breath. Temperance wondered why on earth this foppish nobleman had joined the military and accepted a commission to the rough-and-tumble of Jamestown. More perplexing was his success. Though not originally selected to serve on the Virginia council, he had become instrumental early on, scoring successes against the Indians, leading expeditions along the river, and becoming Smith’s trusted officer. Temperance conceded that there must be substance to the pale dandy which did not meet the eye. How else to explain his survival after two years when so many others had perished?

“As you are aware,” he began, “I have instituted rationing. A half can of meal a day should last us through the winter months.” His brown eyes gleamed, the first indication to Temperance of what lurked underneath his frail facade. “I have dispatched Captain Ratcliffe to Orapaks to trade with the Powhatans. Francis West and his men are similarly engaged with the

Patawomecks. We also have our livestock, and abundant game and fish. There is no cause to despair or panic."

"Rationing *and* a feast?" Worth retorted. "There is no sense to be made of it."

"You are free to relinquish your share," Percy said. Worth cleared his throat and looked into his plate.

"I fete you," Percy continued, bearing down on Worth, "for the simple fact that we must remember we are Englishmen." He shifted his gaze to the party at large. "A civilized and prosperous nation can, even in this far-flung colony, provide one proper meal to its countrymen. Else we risk succumbing to the savagery that threatens our way of life. Already," he grew more animated, the color rising in his face and hands, "we have suffered defections." He was speaking of the glassmakers whose desertion was still sorely felt as their skills would have provided obvious benefits. "Worse," he added, "are those who consort with the Indian women." He stopped abruptly, his breath cut short. He wheezed and gasped for air. When Temperance stood to aide him, he held up his hand. "It will pass," he said. Long moments later, all of them watching in distress, his breathing evened out.

As if on cue, the steward and one other servant, a boy just shy of puberty, presented the coup de grâce—the roast pig. The diners gasped and clapped. They had not tasted pork in months, having to wait for the first frost to ensure the meat would not spoil in the Virginia heat. The swine, its mouth agape, rested on a huge wooden platter in the center of the table. It was surrounded by roasted turnips and acorns. The settlers waited, their hands clenched beneath the table, as the steward carefully pulled off crackling and sliced the meat paper thin. Temperance, in anticipation, had to dab daintily at the corners of her mouth. When, at last, she tasted the crispy, fat-saturated skin, she nearly moaned aloud. Others didn't hold back. Percy, she noticed, watched them eagerly, as if doing so increased his gustatory pleasure. Temperance could have eaten half the pig herself, but she quickly spooned her turnips and acorns onto her plate to fill her up. Instead of gobbling down her small allotment of pork, she was able to resist the tyranny of hunger and slip the last remaining shred of skin and flesh she had been served into her pocket.

After the pork came the pheasant and quail. Again, the dinner guests were served mere flakes of the delicate fowls, which were gamy but tender. That was followed by broiled pike and mustard greens. Each course, rather than sate her appetite, seemed to heighten it, as if she felt the need to store as much as she could, not knowing when or if she would ever eat like this again. Saving part of it for Lily was an extraordinary force of will. She was relieved when she was served the corn pudding, because she could not stash it away, and so ate it all down, despite the fact it was a congealed mess, tasteless and lumpy.

When it was over, the plates were cleared and minute portions of a Spanish Medoc served in perhaps the only stemmed glassware in the New World. Temperance and the other guests sat in a stupor. The food had acted on them like a narcotic. Though their stomachs were finally full after months of scarcity, the sensation was one of heaviness. They could not have eaten more had they wanted to. But neither did they want to push themselves away from the table. For a few brief hours they had been able to block out the precariousness of their lives. And though Percy's gesture was clearly excessive and wasteful, it was also a reprieve.

***

Lily held the long, smooth pole in her hands and peered into the water coursing over her feet. The shallow edge of the riverbank was not ideal for fishing, but without a boat or canoe, she had no other choice. She stabbed at the water over and over until she was breathless, cursing the good-for-nothings at Jamestown who had allowed the unthinkable to happen. All fourteen nets set up in the James River to snare fish had rotted. The makeshift weir traps were not far behind, having been constructed of wood rather than stone, which was scarce. "In other words," mistress had said when one of the contrite fishermen delivered the bad news to the settlers, "we are surrounded by water and cannot extract its bounty. And now, winter is nearly upon us." Mistress immediately took to her log to record the debacle while Lily headed to the James, her pole fashioned by the hermit fiddler, who was something of a carpenter when he was not making music.

She had watched the Powhatan on the James, standing upright in their canoes, floating serenely downriver, poles in hand, deftly spearing one fish after another. They made it look so easy she was sure she could catch one or two bass or bluegill. She set her feet shoulder-width apart, held her spear as if she were about to churn butter, and waited for a flash of silver or a darkened shadow to flit by. When something jumped out of the water, she lunged for it, slipping on a slimy rock and plunging into the river. She heard laughter. She fought her way out of the water, then quickly flipped the pole, holding it like a javelin.

"Who's there?" she demanded. Her cap had been dislodged in the fall so that her unpinned hair fell about her shoulders like corn silk. The threadbare bodice, blouse, and skirt she reserved for work clung to her, revealing the contours of her spare frame.

"It is James Owen," he said, stepping out from behind a large cypress. "Put that down. You wouldn't want to skewer me. The fish taste better."

"You followed me," she said, lowering the pole.

"Yes, of course. I wanted to see my handiwork in use. It is the craftsman's vanity." He smiled. The streaks of gold in his coiled hair made him look to her like hidden treasure.

"I told you I was to fish." She became aware of her body, and eyed her jacket flung on the bank, too far to retrieve. She tried to shake out her garments and gather her hair, finally dropping her hands in frustration.

"I had to see for myself how you might do that, with just a pole and unbounded nerve," he said.

She turned her back and waded again into the water. When he came up behind her and put his arms around her, she did not resist. He was warm and smelled like sweet hay. She leaned against him.

"Here," he said, taking hold of the pole. "I've little experience with this, but I'm sure you are not to grab onto it as if harpooning a whale." He spread her hands on the pole, one above the other, and angled it to the surface of the water. They stood close together poised for a kill. Lily could feel his heart beating, slow and even. Hers was racing. His breath tickled her cheek. She struggled to focus on the river. A large school of bluegill brought her to. She instantly jabbed at the water, but felt resistance, as James, trying to help her spear them, was working against her.

"Let go, let go!" she shouted. She felt his hands leave the pole, but by then the fish had vanished. She tried to make chase, stabbing blindly at the water, but it was too late. "There now, you've done it," she said, standing knee-deep in the river.

"There will be more," he said. "Come, let's try again."

"No!" she snapped, surprised at her own gathering fury.

"Go away. I cannot think when you're about." When he stepped toward her, his hand out, she shrieked, "You will be the death of me!" James dropped his hand and walked away.

She watched him retreating and stifled the longing that swept over her. She had not meant to say such a thing to him. And she had not wanted him to leave. It was constant fear which drove her to push him away. She needed the fear, she reasoned, wiping her eyes, to stay alive. But it was small comfort now. She was alone in the great river with little more than a wooden stick to keep her company. She looked in all directions and saw nothing but trees, sky, and water, none of which cared whether she lived or died. Right then she would have given a piece of herself if he would come back and hold her in his arms—even if it meant she would never eat again—and she could simply melt away in the forge of his ardent embrace.

***

William Fettiplace, the second in command, stepped off the pinnace onto the gangplank. The muscular man with the athlete's stride said nothing, keeping his bearing, though he was peaked as butter and his eyes bloodshot. He marched past all the onlookers, those who had rushed to the dock in hopes the supply mission had been successful, including Temperance, who guessed immediately that the men had, once again, come up empty-handed. One young soldier on the boat, Jack Comb, got on all fours, scampering and bleating like a lamb. When his mate Dermer tried to restrain him, he shouted, "We're all of us meat." He laughed hysterically and repeated himself again and again until Dermer punched him unconscious. He then carried him onshore and dumped him on the sandy bank. The spectacle barely diverted the attention of the settlers, who waited anxiously for news from the commander of the ship, John Ratcliffe.

"Where's the cap'n?" someone in the crowd shouted at Dermer. He shook his bowed head.

"Come on, man," Nancy, the seamstress, cajoled. "Give us the news. Are we to be fed?"

Dermer looked into the worried faces of the people. His was the color of chalk, and his eyes were hollowed. Temperance had remembered him as having a thick thatch of salt-and-pepper hair. It was now completely white. She could see he was torn between laying it all down, whatever it was, or turning and running. He began slowly, his voice hoarse and sorrowful.

"It were Powhatan, the chief. In Orapaks," he said. "We was to meet up with him there and trade. The boy, Henry Spelman, set it up, him able to speak their language. He said Powhatan promised venison and corn, a goodly portion, what would keep us in meat and meal for a fortnight, at least. After we anchored the ship near Orapaks, we took a barge to shore near the trading post. When we got there, 'twas as expected. The chief's men greeted us, they did, as friends, and offered us one of the chief's domed huts to stay for the night. The next day, the Powhatans carried us by river to their storehouse. The chief was regal, dressed in fur to fend off the cold, lookin' every bit like a great snowy owl. Cap'n and Powhatan stood off by themselves, and I knew they was bartering fierce. Beads and copper for food. I didn't think it would pass muster. The sailors had already traded so much copper with the Indians, they turned their noses up at it. But here we were with nothing else and yet the chief lookin' jolly pink about it.

"Well, I heard the cap'n and the chief jesting about the ladies and all. 'Will you marry, John Ratcliffe?' the chief asked. 'I do not have enow to choose from,' Cap'n said. 'If rash, I fear I shall make a grave mistake.' The old fox came back quick, and said, 'I have made seven such mistakes. But my bed is warm every night.' When they laughed, I thought it finished. Chief Powhatan waved his hand at his men and they hauled three baskets of corn toward the barge. Ratcliffe eyed the haul and got boilin' mad. Said it weren't a fair trade, and they was being cheated. Like that"—Dermer snapped his fingers—"the Powhatans was gone, vanished.

"We all stood there surely caught in a dream. Somethin' evil loomed, we could feel it. Cap'n ordered us onto the boat. 'What about the venison?' one mate asked. 'Maybe they're bringing us the venison.' Before his words died, the arrows flew at us. We ducked for cover and aimed our matchlocks and pistols at the forest, shootin' up nothin' but pine bark. Our weapons was no good to us, slow and clumsy. The Indians could loose ten arrows afore we reloaded one gun, it took us that long. They smelled it, the Indians, whooping and chortling. It seemed as though they surrounded us, yet the river was to our backs. I felt the hair raise on me scalp and knuckles. They had hawk eyes, the archers did, and hit their marks, 'til near half of us lay dead. The cap'n said to make a run for the barge, but no sooner had he spoke, they was on us, like wolves. We fought as best we could, but we were outnumbered. A gruesome sight it was," he went on, as if duty-bound to bear witness. "The Indians fell on the men and knocked them in the head. One poor gent crawled about with a tomahawk wedged in his scalp, beggin' for someone to finish it. The blood ran and puddled at our feet. The blood of our own countrymen, like so much bilge water."

Dermer shivered violently. Nancy rested her large chafed hands on his shoulders.

"A dozen or so of us managed to scramble onto the barge. The Indians didn't give chase, praise God, but the devils weren't finished with us. Beside the dead English ashore were one still alive: Cap'n Ratcliffe. They had him, they did, and let us know, settin' him out front like a trophy, then tetherin' him to a tree. He was a pathetic sight, stripped naked, bruised and bleedin'. Fettiplace took charge and ordered us to hie, there bein' nothin' we could do for the cap'n except get off a few parting shots. We couldn't get away fast enough. What they did to that man, I've never seen the likes of in all me day, and hope to never ag'in. Out of the woods, the women came, about ten of 'em, the leader carrying a torch. Beautiful they were, tall and brown, like the men, and nearly as strong in their limbs. They was singin' I couldn't tell what. 'Yah, ha, ha, Tewittaw, Tewittaw,' like they was laughin' at us.

"One of the women carried a basket of clam shells. She set it on a large stone while the others piled sticks and leaves close by the cap'n, and set the torch to it. The flames licked the sky. It was hell in a blaze of orange. One of the women, as pretty a piece you'll ever see, what with the eagle feathers in her cape and beads twined in her hair, picked a large shell out of the basket. She held it up to the others, me thinks for approval, then stepped to where the cap'n was lashed to the tree. Quick as a wink, she cut him. He flinched, doin' his best to be brave. When she dragged the shell to scrape the skin from his flesh, he let out a scream that I will hear for the rest of me life. After the devil woman flayed the skin, she threw it into the fire. Then she gave way to the next woman, who had her turn at it. We watched from the stern, not wanting to look but helpless not to. Each woman skinnin' the cap'n alive, until we rowed out of sight. It went on for a good while, it did, for we could see the smoke from the fire a far pace off, and farther than that, we could still hear the screams."

When Dermer was finished, nobody spoke. As if obeying a silent signal, they all turned away from Dermer and trudged back to the fort. Jack Comb, regaining consciousness, gingerly touched the corner of his mouth, and mewled.

***

I have arrived at the juncture in my report where I must decide whether my loyalties are to my second husband, Francis West, or to the truth. To most wives, it is no choice at all, for a woman must at all times be the faithful and loyal helpmeet. I am dangerously at odds in that regard, according to both biblical scripture and English jurisprudence, perhaps because Francis is a man I married for convenience, not love. It is, I admit, no way to enter into a union of souls, but for that, such sentiments in my situation are impractical if not laughable. Still, married I am, and swollen with his child, one I may never know. My attachments, then, are not of the earth, but a heavenly realm where I hope to dwell once I die. There, I am fairly certain, husbands do not reign supreme. And so, because I cannot serve two masters, I choose the truth.

Some may cavil that, in relating this episode, I have not taken the high road. Rather, they will say, I have betrayed Francis and the English for the sake of the Indians. It is not so. I have no particular affection for the natives who turned their backs in our greatest hour of need, who denied us food, tricked and butchered us. They are a hostile enemy, constantly threatening our existence. No, my concerns are not with the Indians; I write for the soul of the English people, who cannot emulate that brutality and heartlessness and still call themselves civilized.

But that is precisely what they did, under the leadership of my husband, the current governor of Virginia. I must purge my own conscience and set the record straight. Though I am no friend of the Indian, it is my moral duty to speak for them in ways they cannot. Their story must also be told and recorded, even if it is through the beclouded lens of an unsympathetic Englishwoman.

Shortly after Captain Ratcliffe and his men were slaughtered at Orapaks, another trading party, led by Francis, met with the Patawomecks at Passapatanzy. These Indians, who lived up the bay on the Potomac, were crafty. A small tribe, they took heed to befriend the English and the Powhatan both, so as to feather their beds. They had ample store, nearly a thousand acres planted in corn along the river, and were well-positioned to strike a hard bargain. Reports conflict as to what happened next. Francis has provided testimony for the public record, which he has repeated to me in private, with some variations meant to reassure me. They did not.

Whilst Francis and the Patawomeck chief, Iopassus, haggled, two of the Indians jostled with the English, belittling the size of their manhood, as men are wont to do. Soon enough, a fight broke out. In the ensuing fray, the two Indians were felled, then, on Francis's command, beheaded. Afraid of full-scale retaliation, Francis ordered his men to take the corn and flee, back to the pinnace, the Swallow. *Once there, the crew, over thirty of them, took matters into their own hands. They refused to return to the fort which they reckoned was doomed. Instead, they sailed back to England, taking with them the much-needed corn and the best boat left in the shrinking fleet.*

Francis was helpless in the face of mutiny. Once in England, he was quickly exonerated of wrongdoing and sent back to Jamestown the following year. He never was held to account for his brutality against the Patawomeck. It bothers me still. On the eve of our wedding, I asked him, "How do you justify such atrocities?" He looked at me with such puzzlement that I might as well have been asking about the beheading of chickens for all it concerned him.

I married Francis in spite of it, because it was expected. The laws of noblesse oblige had caught up with me in Virginia, and, as the widow of one governor, I could not escape the office or the title of another. I had children to raise in a makeshift town perched on a vast river and backed up to a feral continent. God forgive me, for in joining Francis in matrimony, I too am guilty of the sins against the Indians, though I myself did not wield the ax that sent them to an early grave. If it pleases God to smite me, it is right and just. I am contrite and seek absolution the only way I know how—by testifying on behalf of the Indians in the world the English call new, but which is to them ancient. In so doing, I hope to spare my children and my children's children the stain of my transgressions. That is the power and efficacy of truth. It rises from the muck and mire like a wildflower; it is the best of us, and our only hope.

***

Perched in the bulwark, Hugh Pryse kept his birdlike eyes locked on the river. "'Tis damnable slow," he spat to himself, shivering as he leaned against the cast-iron demi-culverin covered in rime. The light of day could not come fast enough. The bulwark offered little protection from the stiff wind that lashed him in the predawn darkness. As soon as the sun peaked over the horizon, he could retreat to his quarters, rustle the day sentry out of the warm cot they shared, and sleep like the dead. He looked forward to waking in the afternoon, then escaping into the forest. Only then would the constriction he constantly felt in his chest ease. Calm would spread through him, his body in motion finally at peace. He would be back to his watch late evening, but until then, he could walk for miles in any direction and feel released from the wrenching sensation that had plagued him from an early age, of being penned in.

The restless third son of landed gentry, he would inherit neither position nor fortune, so he was groomed to apprentice in a print shop, which led to a bleeding ulcer. It had been the reason he had left the relative comforts of home to come to the New World—the promise of unlimited and mostly uninhabited space. His guard duty was a grim irony and a worse fate. But with so few able-bodied men to act as lookouts, he could not beg off. Every night, when dawn was an hour or two away, he felt an uncontrollable urge to leap over the palisades and disappear into the woods for good. But he was not a strong man. Nor was he adept at surviving in the wilderness. For now, he would shadow the English and Indian hunters and fishermen to learn all he could, so that one day he could light out on his own. His dream was to walk from one end of the continent to the other, hoping that he would run out of life before he ran out of land. Until that day arrived, and to keep from deserting his post, he would imagine the forest in his mind's eye and traverse it that way. It kept him grounded, at least until the first gray light of dawn nearly drove him mad with anticipation.

As he peered east toward the horizon, he spotted a canoe in the mist rising from the icy river. It was not unusual. The Indians fished almost daily, and often at dawn, or traveled the river to various trading posts. Six other canoes emerged from the wispy fog and, instead of drifting by, formed a semicircle in front of the fort. Hugh stood up straight. He fumbled with his snaphaunce, making sure it was primed to fire, then rushed to the opposite side of the bulwark. He thought of shouting to Henry Collins, who manned the bulwark to the west, but was afraid of needlessly disturbing the slumbering settlement. He shot back across the bulwark and was hit by the first brilliant rays of the sun rising above the river. It blinded him momentarily. He closed his eyes and turned inland. When he opened them again, he could not distinguish the sun spots from the dark figures he saw amassing in the forest behind the fort. When he realized what he was witnessing, the desire to escape his post was never greater, but to do so would be suicide, for on all sides, and from every vantage point, Jamestown was surrounded.

***

"We are besieged," George Percy announced from the rudimentary pulpit of the church. He stood tall but listless. Behind him were the council members, rumpled and disheveled, having leapt out of their beds when Hugh Pryse sounded the alarm. They had quickly organized a party to meet the Indians, in hopes the dawn visitation was perhaps a peace offering, or a ceremony with which they were not familiar. The plume of arrows and blood-curdling war cries sent the men scurrying back to the safety of the fort.

Temperance, still drugged from sleep, sat next to Lily on the crammed bench. She had endured yet another nightmare in which snakes of all sizes appeared wherever she walked, out of doors and in her home. One of them bit her in the side. She woke plagued by sharp pains in her bowels. Percy's frightening news seemed more dreamlike than her encounter with the snakes. It was not until she surveyed the pinched and distraught faces of the settlers that his words sunk in. Her pain intensified. When she winced and doubled over, Lily put her hand on her back.

"Mistress?"

"It's nothing. I'm bound. It will pass after I eat something."

"I will make some fennel broth," Lily said.

Temperance nodded, waiting for the spasm to run its course.

"It appears," Percy went on, slowly, "the Indians have encircled us."

"Are we under attack?" asked the logger, who sat next to Temperance. He smelled perpetually of pine, as if his spiky beard were made of loblolly needles instead of hair.

"No," Percy answered. "Else we would have already been set upon. They clearly hold back."

"But why?" asked a young lemon-haired boy of ten or eleven. He stood against the wall, his mouth agape. "What are they waitin' for? I'll have at 'em." His mother, an older version of her cheeky son, yanked him by the arm and lightly slapped his head.

"They're starvin' us!" Nancy shouted. Her words rang out in the crowded church. They were met with silence.

Cord stood up, hat in hand. Spike sat at his feet, his pointed ears alert. "The fields, Master Percy?" he asked, ashen and jittery. "We've still the last of the fall harvest. It isn't much, just the late squash and beans we planted with corn."

"It is too great a risk. We will watch and wait," Percy said, clearly annoyed with questions he could not answer. "The natives will tire and leave us be."

"So we do nothing?" Temperance said. The pain gave her the courage to speak. Many of the settlers echoed her disbelief.

A commotion outside the gates startled the already skittish gathering. Someone, a man, was banging on the gates, dull thuds made with bare fists. He shouted and shrieked, beseeching God. A woman, Anne Laydon, whispered "John" to herself, as if thinking aloud, and pushed her way out of the crowded church. Two men followed. The rest of the settlers spilled outdoors into the common area. They banded together, many of them locking arms, as their only protection from the threat that engulfed them. When the gates flew open, an arrow shot into the fort. The cooper, a wiry Welshman with a mop of black hair, ducked in time. The arrow sailed into the arm of a girl holding her newborn son, the fourteen-year-old wife of the middle-aged Polish brewer. She fell to the ground in a dead faint, maintaining her tight grip on her son. Lily ran to her. She gently eased the baby out of the mother's arms and called to Nancy, closest to her, to sit with the girl and child. As Nancy knelt down heavily beside them, Lily raced across the commons.

Arrows clattered against the fort like hail. The gates closed quickly behind John Laydon. He stumbled into the commons, his doublet open and cockeyed and his white linen shirt torn along the sleeve. He fell to his knees, one of them bleeding, relieved and gasping for air. Though arrows were lodged in the gates like quills of a porcupine, Laydon was unharmed. Temperance marveled at his good fortune. He had somehow managed to make it back alive, perhaps because he had an age-old reason to do so. He was one of the few married men in the settlement. Anne Laydon, who had arrived with the Second Supply as Mistress Forest's servant girl, was the first bride in the New World. She nearly knocked her husband down embracing him with her ample arms. She held onto John for a few moments, crying, and kissing his matted hair. The settlers watched, spellbound.

"Speak up, man. What news?" Percy demanded, having made his way through the crowd.

"I have come from Hog Island. Escaped is more like it," he said, still struggling for air. "They're all gone. Slaughtered."

"Who?" Percy asked. "Who are all gone?" His brown eyes flashed terror. Temperance cursed his lack of restraint, which could lead to panic.

"The swine."

The settlers gasped, as if it had been people instead of pigs that had perished. Temperance realized that in some ways, news of human death would have been preferable. Laydon shook his head, kept it bowed. He had been tending the herd at Hog Island, where they grazed, when it was overtaken by Indians. Laydon had hid behind a bald cypress. While the Indians were reveling in the slaughter, he stole one of their canoes. He crossed the river to Jamestown, spotting the small embargo in time to shift course downstream, beach his canoe and slip through a narrow breach in the siege between the Indians on the river and those ashore. They had spotted him just yards from the fort, and peppered him with arrows, all of which had, miraculously, missed their mark. When he had finished his report, Anne placed both her hands on her abdomen and closed her eyes in prayer. John gently laid his hand atop hers and lowered his head.

The Polish brewer's wife came to, screaming for her baby. Nancy shushed her in a gentle voice. The girl appeared oblivious to the arrow lodged deeply in her arm, stretching it out to the slumbering child in Nancy's arms. She screamed louder until Lily, having rushed back, spoke to her quietly, smoothing her brassy hair. She had gone to fetch some rum from their meager supply, along with honey, a rag, and a pair of shears, which she now placed on the ground.

"You're Sarah, aren't you?" Lily asked the girl.

"Yes," she said, her teeth clenched.

"What's your baby's name, then?" she asked.

"Harry."

"You can't hold Harry proper like this, can you?"

Sarah shook her head. Lily gently laid the girl's pierced arm in her lap, and with the shears clipped off the feathered end of the shaft.

"Hold your breath," she said evenly, barely concealing the tremor in her voice. She gathered herself and, lifting Sarah's arm up and away from her, clutched the shaft. Temperance noticed her hesitation and wondered why she tarried pulling it out. Instead, with one firm thrust, Lily pushed down on the arrow and through the arm. She heard a chorus of "ohs" as Sarah howled. It woke Harry, who commenced to wail.

"Sing," Lily said to Nancy.

"Me?" Nancy jostled the shrieking baby. "It would scare the lad worse."

"It can't get any worse."

Nancy started into a lullaby, her voice deep and cracked and woefully out of tune. She stroked the baby's head with her sure fingers. Harry grew quiet, smiling.

"I'll be," Nancy whispered. "He's got no ear for the melody, like me!"

As Nancy sang, Lily quickly doused the wound with rum, pressed the rag on it until the bleeding slowed, then slathered it with honey. Afterward, she bound it tightly. Nancy eased Harry into her mother's arms and patted Lily's back. When Lily stood up, her attention still on her patient, the settlers gave way.

"Well done," someone said.

"Ye saved her," said another.

Admiring eyes, which she could not meet, followed her. Instinctively, she reached into her pocket. There, Temperance knew, was the crucifix, which Lily would clutch only after she felt deserving of its blessings.

THE RECKONING

DECEMBER 1609

George Percy and the council members took account of our supplies, what was left of them. They did their best, I admit, at keeping all two hundred of us apprised of our situation. After a thorough inventory witnessed by three council members, Percy called us together and laboriously ticked off every ounce of corn meal, dried beans, cured meat, and fish in the storehouse. Under ordinary circumstances, such a litany would have induced yawns and impolite sighs; this had the effect of a barrister reading a will. We listened as if our lives depended on it, which they did. Percy drove this point home. Anyone caught hoarding or thieving would be executed.

Percy then did something remarkable. He instituted mandatory thrice-weekly church attendance, as prescribed by the Book of Common Prayer. Before, the terms of worship had been dutifully observed; now they were required. Normally, I would have balked at such an imposition. Yet, I understood. Percy wished to create a diversion that doubled as fellowship. Many grumbled, especially those who professed no religion. I suspected the crypto-Catholics were not amused either, having to triple their weekly deceptions as pious Protestant worshippers. But the unexpected happened. The church, which I had been loath to support, even from a young age, became something else. In the first week after the siege, a forgettable sermon was followed by voices raised in prayer and then, song. I had experienced these services before, many times, yet on this occasion, perhaps because the stakes were so high, the obligatory became the transcendent. Our incantations were thrilling to the soul, not because they spoke the language of religious orthodoxy but because they acted in unison. If we were to die in such a horrible fashion, we would do so together rather than apart. Perhaps that is the true mission of the church, not a body that teaches us how to live, so much as it prepares us to die. With no industry to occupy us and ample leisure to become the devil's playthings, we may have wiped one another out long ere we starved to death. In this sanctuary, we were saved from ourselves.

Having done so much to secure us from within, Percy's next move should have been to chase off the threats from without. But as the days, then weeks went by, it was apparent he had no intention of dispatching a party to breech the embargo and find food. We had ample men, many of them soldiers recently returned from two failed outposts. The third, Point Comfort at Algernon, led by Captain Davis, was garrisoned with about thirty men. They still stood, for all we knew, and thus, if alerted, could constitute a stealth show of force against the Powhatan siege. I said as much to Percy, as tactfully as I could. He had not rebuffed me and so I was buoyed. And yet, more weeks passed and Percy continued to do nothing. I prayed it was a temporary stay, and that his extreme caution would give way to a more adventurous spirit. Hopefully, before we ran out of food.

In the meantime, my conversations with George increased in earnest. I spoke to him of the suffocating siege, of Percy's timidity, of starvation rattling our gates. Other times, I'd regale him with the mundane, how Lily darned the hole in my last pair of woolen socks with loose threads from the hem of her skirt. Or how, when the first snow fell, the settlers gathered in the commons and tilted their heads back, mouths agape, like a nest of starlings. There were choice bits of gossip. "George," I'd whisper in the empty church library, "it is said lay preacher Ford is smitten with Chief Powhatan's third wife! Oh, and Nancy is convinced Mistress Collins is with child!" Sometimes in response I could hear George's voice, strong but laced with a sweetness, as if the edges of his words were sanded to a pleasant roundness. His laughter, too, visited me on rare occasions, rising as it did from deep in his belly, then lodging in his throat. More often than not, I was met with silence. On those occasions, in fits of grief and despair, I lashed out. "Here I sit whilst you are asleep in the ocean. What say you now about my chances?" I suppose by taunting him I hoped to somehow conjure his presence. In keeping him alive in my mind's eye, I kept myself alive if for nothing else than sheer hubris. I had survived contrary to all expectations, including his. It was cold comfort, but comfort nevertheless. I clung to it, then planned for spring, fully intending either rescue or liberation.

***

Priscilla knew that Henry Collins had not meant to backhand her. It clearly pained him to see her on the floor of their quarters, where she lay crumbled and crying. He prided himself on his pretty little wife, with white-blond hair and rosy cheeks, easily bruised he discovered.

"Are you so grievously injured?" he asked, anxiously. "I barely touched you."

She kept her hand over her burning cheek and split lip. It might incite him more to see that he had left a mark.

"How far along are you?" he asked, visibly trying to contain his rage. Sound carried in the fort, especially on a bone-cold night when wind and water were uncharacteristically still.

"Three months, me thinks." She stared at the floor.

He paced around the small room. The embers of the fire cast a reddish glow across his face. He had fine blond hair the texture of tassels, and bright blue eyes. Slim and boyish, he and Priscilla could have been brother and sister. Henry had been a middling actor in London where he played mostly female roles, before he was chased out for skimming the gate receipts. They had met on the Third Supply and married soon after setting foot in Jamestown.

Priscilla slowly pushed herself into a sitting position. She watched Henry out of the corner of her eye as he paced. She knew enough to wait for his fury to die down, or for him to storm out, as he often did, to seek out the soldiers playing at dice or gambling. He'd entertain them with scenes from popular tragedies, often switching effortlessly between roles. Afterward, he'd stumble home in the wee hours of the morning, drunk with praise and the rum the men plied him with as payment for the performance. But the rum, which the soldiers had scored in the West Indies, was nearly gone. Henry would have performed for free, though without the strong spirits, the men grew churlish and quarrelsome, having no patience for unfavorable rolls of the dice let alone long-winded soliloquies delivered by a third rate actor.

"Pray, husband," she said. "Dost thou not have charity? It is our child." Priscilla's lower lip quivered. She was just turned fifteen, and had never had a finger laid on her, until now. It was a strange and sickening sensation.

"Are you stupid as well as improvident?" he shouted. "You have done this to increase your rations."

"I shall eat only what I need. Thou art sick with fear. The Bible sayeth—"

"Fie on the Bible, foolish girl." He drew his hand back, as if to hit her again. "Jesus is a chimera—one your father and his rascally brethren used to fleece the masses." He kicked at the chair and shoved the table across the room.

Priscilla put her hands to her ears. She longed for her father, a man whose London congregation had deemed a saint. He had raised her alone after Priscilla's mother died giving birth to her, and he never remarried. Rather than revile or blame her, as some bereft widowers are wont to do, he cherished his only child, pampering her with unconditional love and a first-rate education. When he was approached by the Virginia Company to replace Rev. Hunt at Jamestown, he had asked Priscilla's permission first. She leapt at the opportunity, embracing her father's missionary vision of spreading the word of God amongst the Indians. But early in the voyage, her father, like so many others, took sick and died. She had nearly jumped in after him when the pallbearers tilted the wooden plank on which her father lay and emptied him into the sea.

At first, she was inconsolable. Then, as the wracking grief subsided, she felt adrift and frightened. She had lost her anchor and her compass, never having lived a single day without her father's loving guidance. She did not know who she was without him, or what she could become. Into this vacuum stepped Henry, whose angelic good looks, silvery tongue, and genteel manners she mistook for virtue. When he proposed two weeks after her father's death, she was so grateful, she accepted on the spot. It was well before he backhanded her to the floor that she knew she had made a terrible mistake.

"Stop your whimpering!" He pulled her hands away from her ears. "It rankles me."

"Thou dost blaspheme, Henry. It is an offense to God."

"You are an offense to me. You and that bastard child."

"What sayest thou? I am a true wife."

He kicked her. She cried out, then scuttled to the far end of the room near the cold hearth.

"Thou mayest lose wife and child if thou dost not change thy ways," she said, drawing into a ball.

He reached for his cape on the peg and tossed it theatrically across his shoulder. With one last withering look, he held forth. "If I do lose thee," he began, in the stage voice she knew so well, "I do lose a thing / That none but fools would keep." He unlatched the door and walked out into the frigid night. His words, which she recognized from Shakespeare's *Measure for Measure*, echoed in her head. She and her father had loved the great dramatist, attending many a play together at the Globe. It was yet one more treasure her father had given her that Henry managed to twist into something sordid. Priscilla gathered herself from the floor, set the table and chairs right, then retrieved her Bible from the cedar chest. She turned to Psalms and began to sing, to her deceased mother and father, and to her unborn child.

***

As the makeshift coffin was laid in the ground, Temperance averted her eyes. It was not the first burial she had witnessed, but it was the most personal. There had been many deaths at sea, and since her arrival in Jamestown, it had become a nearly weekly occurrence. The news often spread through the settlement before the church sexton, Hal Avery, could don his black robe and make his way through town clanging the iron bell. It was a forlorn sound, as it meant their numbers were further reduced. Temperance had grown remarkably adept at dismissing the mounting evidence of her own fragile mortality, including the rotted smell that clung to everything, including her hair. Those who had perished, she reasoned, were weaklings or old or sickly or reckless. But Nancy's death was a shock. The robust and feisty seamstress had been washing clothes in her outdoor tub when she keeled over, face first into the sudsy water. By the time Cord ran over, she was dead, the surprise on her face frozen for eternity. "Her heart's gave out," Cord announced, though no postmortem exam was performed nor a cause of death issued. There would be no point. Nancy was dead and that was that.

Temperance's carefully spun cocoon of denial unraveled as she listened to the thud of dirt cover the coffin and Hal Avery's sonorous recital of the twenty-third Psalm. The oldest man left at Jamestown, perhaps fifty, he held his Bible at arm's length, in order to read the words. Temperance averted her eyes from the grave and surveyed the mourners, nearly every settler in the fort. She saw the fear that she herself felt. If Nancy had been felled, they all could be. She pushed the thought away. Unlike so many of the others who had died, Nancy was no stranger to them. Sought after on a daily basis, the seamstress had probably repaired at least one garment worn by every person in the settlement. It afforded the lowly seamstress an uncommon measure of prestige, entrusted as she was with the scant clothing the settlers relied on to shield themselves from the elements. In covering their nakedness Nancy made herself indispensable. Settlers suffered her sharp tongue because they knew it came with a skillful needle. She might bark all she wanted as long as she completed the delicate stitch that not only preserved a precious item of clothing but also a vestige of the civilization they had left behind.

Yet Nancy would most likely be forgotten, a crude wooden crucifix the only marker of her expertise, and of her courage and fortitude in braving the New World. Temperance eyed George Percy, erect, self-important, and entitled. He would be enshrined in the annals of Jamestown records, Nancy would not. Her grief and fear turned to anger. Temperance realized she might also suffer the same fate—a short, brutish life and an anonymous grave. Percy, after all, had already dismissed her counsel, as if even alive she were of little import. Temperance vowed it would not happen again.

A cold wind blew in from the river, rattling the bare branches of the few sycamores and tulip poplars still standing in the fort. It roared and howled, as if the Powhatans, grown tired of their vigil, were on the attack. The mourners clutched their caps and held down their capes, not letting the wind distract them from the burial. Hal Avery, grimly patient, waited for the gust to die down, then finished the psalm. Afterward, he bowed his head, Bible in hand, as one by one the bereaved settlers said their silent goodbyes to Nancy and walked away. Avery and Percy were the last to leave. They watched as the gravediggers patted the dirt in place and planted the unvarnished cross. Temperance waited to confront Percy, overhearing Avery mention how it was a blessing that the ground was not yet frozen. Percy nodded, then he too left. Temperance quickly followed.

"Master Percy," she said, raising her voice. He stopped and looked at her as if trying to place her.

"It is Temperance Flowerdew," she said, craning her neck to make eye contact.

"I know who you are." He smiled slightly, though there was no warmth in it. His face was ashen and his brown eyes protruded unnaturally. "It has not been that long since our last conversation."

"The seamstress, Nancy, it is a sad day," she said, to break the ice.

"She will be missed," he said. "I pray you are well, mistress."

"As well as can be expected."

They stood for a moment in silence. Percy looked at his timepiece hooked to his belt, then cleared his throat.

"Are you . . . are we prepared to . . ." she stammered.

He cocked his head, in anticipation. Temperance sensed that he was amused. She felt the all-too-familiar burn well up in her.

"I have a plan," she said in a rush.

"You. Have a plan?"

"Yes. To nullify the siege."

Percy raised an eyebrow.

"You have spent time on these weighty issues," he said, dryly.

A blast of wind knocked her white cap back. Strands of glossy black hair slipped out and whipped her in the face. It made her feel young and undignified. She tried to regain some advantage. "What else of import is there to think about, Master Percy?" she asked. "Our next banquet?"

"You are impertinent." His smile faded. He drew in a raspy breath of air.

"I am desperate, sir. We should all be desperate."

"Desperation is a poor taskmaster. Would you risk lives?" he asked quietly, as if speaking to a small child.

"We risk lives by doing nothing." She kept her voice calm, but she could feel her body throb with impatience.

"And you are an expert on governance?"

"No. And neither am I a fool."

"And yet a woman who deigns to speak to me so boldly," he said. His breathing became more labored.

"A woman indeed," she said, holding back the salvos she longed to launch at this spineless aristocrat who cared more about the starch in his ruff than the empty bellies of his charges. He had no more business governing an outpost than Nancy did, though Temperance would have cast her lots with the seamstress as far more likely to pull them out of this quagmire. "Then it should not impugn your superior sensibilities to hear what I have to say."

"Get on with it, woman. You have squandered my goodwill. I listen now only because I am a gentleman." He began to wheeze. She waited for him to catch his breath.

"It is very simple," she said, quickly. "Select our most able-bodied men and disguise them as Powhatans."

She watched him start in confusion. Then she saw the light of understanding in his bulging eyes. It gave her courage to go on.

"We are all well-acquainted with the Powhatan dress and have the means to replicate it. The face paint would be easy enough, and the deerskin and weapons we have confiscated from dead Indians. We could cover the men's pale skin with mud. From a far distance, such a deception might fool the enemy for a short time, enough to quickly gather some sustenance from the fields. The risk is real, but, I believe, the rewards could be our salvation."

She saw a flicker of hope in Percy's face.

"How would we dispatch the men to and from the fort without the Powhatans making the discovery?" he asked, as if speaking now to an advisor.

"Under cover of darkness."

"And if they are caught?"

"Several of our men speak the language. One of the translators could attempt to negotiate a trade."

Percy laughed.

"We have nothing to trade."

"We have everything to lose." She met his eyes, which flashed a rare moment of accord. "If the English and Powhatans negotiate face to face, there is always the opportunity for a treaty. Human nature is so constituted as to remain at each other's throats for only so long."

She waited for him to acknowledge the viability of the plan. She knew John Smith would have.

"It simply will not do," he said flatly.

"You jest."

"I will not allow the men to demean themselves with such a dishonorable ruse. I would rather we all perish than for loyal subjects of the British crown to reduce themselves to savages."

Temperance looked at him in disbelief. He spoke with conviction, but his reasoning was absurd. The English had enjoyed all manner of Indian culture, from the cuisine, the jewelry, to agriculture, hunting, fishing, and foraging. Some of the men had even taken their women for wives. Percy's reluctance to permit a simple charade that might save their lives meant only one thing. He was afraid. It was easier and safer for Percy to wait out the siege rather than try to do something about it.

"There is no dishonor in staying alive," she said, furious. The burn was getting the best of her, but she didn't care.

"At any cost? Surely not. Next you would have our women cavort about as Indians!" He coughed and wheezed.

"For God's sake, Percy!"

"Hold your tongue, mistress. You forget yourself."

"Set aside your pride."

"Pride pulls us back from the abyss."

"We are already there!" she shouted.

He bent in half, until his struggle for air subsided, then straightened.

"The Indians would see through the masquerade ere the gates had shut behind our men. It serves no purpose."

"But—"

He held up a long finger. "Concealing the skin and moving about in the night might suffice to provide cover. A few hours is all the men would need to gather some sustenance."

"Then you'll do it?" she asked, her hopes rising again.

"I shall think on it." He turned and left her.

"Time is running out!"

He slowed a moment, then resumed his pace. Temperance stood alone, Nancy, and the thirty or so other settlers, already beneath the ground.

***

As if even the heavens were reduced to rationing, the meager snow flurries that floated from the sky on Christmas day afforded little comfort to the parched earth, or the outstretched hands and tongues on which they landed. Lily had set out her buckets, hoping to collect as much of it as she could, since the town well was running dry. She had also hoped to catch sight of James Owen, whom she had not seen since that day at the river, to wish him a Merry Christmas. But he was nowhere about, and his fiddle was silent. She had been taught to capture rain and snow by her father, who had used it to make ale. The secret to brewing, he had told her, was in the water. He had experimented with salt water, but it was too briny. Well water contained stubborn minerals that could not be filtered out. The river, polluted with all manner of waste, just would not do. That left the rain, which he said was God's secret ingredient for the best lager in Sussex County.

She had aspirations back in August, when they had first arrived at the settlement, to set up her own still, as a way to relive her fondest memories of her father. He brewed twice a year, which kept him homebound from his work in the countryside, at least for a few days at a time. She relished his presence, so unlike her mother's. Where she was quiet and neat and always smelled like lavender, he clomped and cursed and carried the scent of fresh tobacco. When he was home there were more spats, but also more laughter. He and Lily's mother could flare up at each other in a heartbeat. The next minute they would nuzzle like otters, chirping and blissful.

The still, while a good excuse to spend time with his family, was no hobby. It kept the family in ale, which was the only safe thing to drink because the water was filthy. Her father also sold his surplus, highly prized in their village, bringing in much-needed cash. He had insisted early on that Lily learn the craft so that if all else failed, she could make a living as a brewer. When she turned seven, Lily was given the time-consuming task of foraging for raw materials. She had to gather the hops from wild vines that grew in the woods. She located and identified the bitter berries that gave ale its edge. She also was to keep an eye on the barley—which her father put in the makeshift kiln to sprout and dry—alerting him when it was ready. At this point, her father's other duties gave way to the brewing process. He'd set the barley to soak, wait a few hours, take a whiff, and declare it properly soused. From there on in, Lily was bound to his side. She watched him as he strained the liquid from the barley and added it to the hops in the kettle to boil. He'd then cool the concoction, and, like an itinerant alchemist, sprinkle in mysterious amounts of yeast and sugar, all the while stirring it with a slotted ladle. Sometimes, he allowed Lily to stir. She reveled in the sharp and bitter smells the brewing released, and in her father's warm hands covering hers when she grew weary and could no longer stir.

She yearned to brew in the New World. But, gazing at the forlorn flakes barely wetting the oaken bucket, she knew it was not yet possible. She had thought of substituting the river for rain, and corn for barley, but while one was plentiful, the other was scarce and she could not risk wasting it. She lifted her face into the soft smattering of snow and laughed softly. The parting gifts bestowed by her mother and father were as different as they were. Mistress would have called them the sacred and the profane. From her mother she received a crucifix, a popish icon she had been compelled to hide so as not to be accused of being a Catholic, which in some ways, at least to the Puritans, was worse than the accusation of witch. From her father, she received a flask, containing his finest lager, laced with three times the alcohol she had been allowed as a child. She knew the gifts were symbols of how she could protect herself from spiritual and financial ruin. The crucifix she caressed daily, but she had saved the beer for a special occasion. It was Christmas. She didn't know how many others she might have. She could think of no better time to drink it, or a better person than mistress to share it with. The beer alone, loaded with nutrients, would fill them up. It would make them merry and warm, to boot. It was the Eucharist, of sorts, this yuletide toast, courtesy of the father.

THE NEW YEAR

JANUARY 1610

The weather turned bitter cold. It had the deleterious effect of keeping everyone indoors, unable to avail themselves of fresh air and daily exercise. Except for Hugh Pryse, who could be seen flitting about with some unknown purpose from one apex of the fort to another at all hours of the day and night. He had taken to talking to himself, flailing his arms as if in a one-sided debate. Temperance knew it had sorely disappointed the girls who, initially beguiled by his genteel background and elegance, now shook their heads and kept their distance.

His behavior was certainly odd, but not unique. At the start of the cold snap, Cord hacked at the frozen ground with his hoe, as if hoping to unearth an undiscovered potato or carrot. When he nearly lost his right hand to frostbite he quit, instead frequenting the smithy where he reshaped his farming tools from dawn to dusk. Spike took to spinning in circles in an effort to halt Cord's disturbing fixations. Henry Collins, meanwhile, stood in the commons and recited Shakespeare or Marlowe, until the settlers, fed up with the racket, ran him off to his pregnant wife. George Percy himself fell to the floor during church services, writhing and foaming. The congregation had at first assumed he was in the grips of the rapture, but it turned out he was seizing. The president had epilepsy. Many of the settlers attributed the onset to the relentless cold and refused to return to church, afraid the governor, always in attendance, might subject them yet again to an unnerving spectacle.

So it was that, other than the wanderlust of Hugh Pryse, the only movement in the beleaguered fort was the occasional settler scurrying out of a warm abode to empty a chamber pot or fetch more firewood. There was also the sexton, forced to venture out more frequently now and ring the dreaded bell. The windswept commons under the unbroken gray skies more than resembled a graveyard—it had become one.

"The fiddler does not play," Temperance said. She and Lily sat in front of the fireplace, sewing a patchwork quilt. It satisfied them both. Lily could use her hands in purposeful ways, and Temperance kept her mind agile, carefully piecing together the fabric into a geometric design. Lily had collected the rags, old clothes, and bedding from the storehouse, where the belongings of the growing number of deceased piled up. It took little persuasion for the superstitious clerk to hand over the goods, which he considered bad luck. Temperance had surveyed the raw materials and sketched out a pattern, the triangular shape of the fort. Neither she nor Lily had any experience with quilt making. But it gave them something to do other than think about food.

"Lily," Temperance said, "the fiddler?"

Lily focused on a scrap of soft cotton, a faded blue. When she held it to her eyes, Temperance realized she was crying. She got up from her chair, gently laying down her square of fabric, and put her hands on Lily's shoulders.

"What is it, dear friend? You frighten me."

"I have not seen James in a month."

"So long? How have you avoided him? Or he you? We are packed in here like the denizens of Bedlam."

"Aye." Lily laughed softly. "And just as crazy." She used the cotton to wipe away her tears. "We had a falling out, James and me. I drove him off. I fear he won't forgive me."

Temperance smiled. Her own longing had led to intimacies with an imagined George Yeardley, in hopes the actual one might eventually materialize. But he never arrived. How lucky Lily was that her James was close by and merely irked at her, rather than vanished. She need only seek him out to quell her yearning. For Temperance, summoning George became increasingly more difficult, his honest blue eyes the only vivid feature of an increasingly shadowy specter. She still confided in him regularly, but he rarely answered now, his voice faint but urgent, like a trumpet from a distant battlefield. She felt him drifting away, her powers of imagination too taxed by hunger and hopelessness to keep a dead man alive.

"He will get past it, Lily." Temperance tried to shake off her gloom. "After all, it is not as if women here are as bountiful as the oysters. He cannot forbear too long or he will lose his pearl to another."

"That's kind of you, mistress. But it's more than that. He does not play. I fear he is sick."

She envied Lily and her beau who yet had a chance.

"I shall pay him a visit."

"No, no!" Lily stood up, spilling her portion of the quilt on the floor. "He will see through that."

Temperance held Lily's arms. "Do you not realize," she said slowly, "that the time for frippery has passed?" She looked into Lily's face, startled by how gaunt and drawn she looked. Her clear eyes were glassy. "We survive each day by the grace of God. Tomorrow is not guaranteed. Would that you waste even one more precious hour in a farce of your own making." She let go of Lily and turned to the fire.

"What if James . . ." Lily stopped. Temperance braced herself. "What if he does not want me?" she asked.

Temperance closed her eyes in relief. She was sure Lily was about to ask if the fiddler, like George, were dead. The thought had occurred to her.

"Enough," she said. "You are the one who pushed him away. It is you who must make amends." Temperance spoke harshly, as if to her own foolish self.

"How? I don't know what to do."

"Neither do I." Temperance laughed. "It is an art my mother gave up teaching me. But come, we shall learn together." She reached for their capes and hats from the peg on the wall. Lily hung back.

"You tarry still?" Temperance asked.

"He will shun me."

"He will fall to his knees in gratitude. Trust me." She draped Lily's cape across her thin shoulders. "Men are not that complicated." She snuffed out the candle and unlatched the heavy door. As she held it open the damp cold air and moonlight flooded the room. Lily stayed rooted.

"Either you do this with me or I shall have a word with him on my own terms. It is your choice."

Lily skulked across the room and followed Temperance.

Together they walked quickly and passed the soldiers playing cards in the smithy. Though night had barely fallen, they would be gaming until first light. Then, with little else to do, they would sleep most of the day, rousing and grumbling about hunger and lice and the rats and the cold. Hunched together in their tattered clothes and unkempt beards, lit by the lurid red glow of the fire-pit, they appeared to Temperance like the condemned in one of Dante's circles of hell.

It took them a scant few minutes to reach the men's barracks.

"Which one is it?" Temperance asked.

Lily shrugged her shoulders. There were doors to six rooms, all lit by torches in sconces. One of them was decorated with a black wreath. Underneath it, leaning against the doorjamb, was a fiddle and a bow. Lily cried out, and rapped on the door until she heard someone stir.

"Who's there?" A man's voice, full of sleep, barked from inside.

"I wish to see the fiddler," Lily said, almost frantically. "Is he about?"

The door flew open. A baldheaded man with a scar along his cheek stood rubbing his eyes. Temperance recognized him as Richard Lyle, the cooper who had of late been conscripted for sentry duty. "I've a watch in a few hours and I need me sleep. What's this racket about the fiddler?" He wore a crumpled hemp shirt, open at the neck, and stained breeches. His legs and feet were bare. The inside of the apartment was dark and dank, smelling like wet wool.

"Is he alive?" Lily's voice pitched.

The man looked from Temperance to Lily as if in a dream.

"Alive?" he asked, scratching his chin.

Temperance pointed at the wreath.

"Nay, nay," he scowled. "That's for Reese Jones, what give up the ghost a week ago. I suppose it's about time I took that down."

Lily and Temperance sagged with relief.

"I would as lief it had been Owen in Reese's stead. That knave has ruined me sleep with his blasted fiddling. I told him if he didn't stop I'd bust it o'er his head, then I'd bust him in two." Richard demonstrated with his fists, squeezing and then snapping an imaginary bow, or neck. "There's the rascal now."

Lily and Temperance spun around. James had come from behind the barracks. He wore no coat or cape and his wiry hair was matted. He appeared ready to dodge them, but it was too late.

"Mistress Flowerdew." He bowed, shivering violently, and kept his eyes on her.

"Master Owen," she said, smiling. He looked wounded and aggrieved. Lily kept her head down. Temperance felt a sudden urge to bolt and let the two of them work out their problems alone. Damnable business, she thought. "We gave you up for dead, sir," she said. "It is a relief to see you above ground." Very deft, she thought to herself, cringing.

James's eyes flickered at Lily. She studied her hands.

"I am sorry to have worried you, mistress, and delighted that you find my beating heart a blessing." He bowed again. "Does your girl share your sentiments?"

"She speaks for herself."

Lily nodded, but still refused to look at James. Temperance sighed. The night was getting longer and colder. She felt her toes going numb in her thin shoes.

"I have missed your music-making. It is a rare pleasure in these dark times."

"Not to everyone."

"The cooper is a bully with potatoes for ears."

"I do not refer to the cooper. I myself cannot bear to play."

Lily flinched and shifted her feet.

"We all suffer, then, for your silence," Temperance said. She turned to Lily, her eyes beseeching her to take the lead.

"And does your girl suffer too?" James asked

"As I have said, she speaks for herself."

Lily nodded again.

"It appears she does not speak at all," James said, lifting his hands in the air. "She has lost her tongue. And a sharp one it was. I bleed still."

"I pray that she will recover it soon, sharp or not," Temperance said between chattering teeth, "ere we all are frozen stiff." She wrapped her arms around her torso, to keep in warmth.

"Yea, mistress, it is a cold night made worse by a wintry heart." He blew warm air into his cupped hands. "I see no reason to stand about waiting for a thaw."

"It is your heart that is ice!" Lily blurted out. "You are bent on punishing me."

"I?" James looked incredulous. "You have exiled me!"

Temperance wanted to say they were all exiled, making James's claims superfluous if not silly, but she was so pleased the two were talking to each other she stayed quiet.

"Where? Where would you go in this godforsaken place that I would not see you for weeks on end?"

"I stay in the storehouse cellar."

"Yes, to punish me."

"You think too well of yourself. Percy has asked me to take up residence in the cellar to stop the filching. I am quite pleased to do so. It is clean and warm. The cooper on the other hand," he pointed his thumb at the apartment, "stinks. I cannot bear it."

Temperance and Lily looked at each other and started to laugh.

"And you are here tonight, why?" Lily asked. "To get another whiff?"

"No, no," Temperance gasped, clutching her sides, "he is here to collect the cooper's clothes. Percy has commissioned them as a secret plan to repel the Indians!"

Lily and Temperance whooped.

"I come here to collect my fiddle and bow," he fumed, "which the cooper has seen fit to finally return to me." He picked up his instrument and cradled it. "You ladies, on the other hand, make me the jape." He turned away from them and stormed off. The sight of him walking away sobered Lily.

"Wait!" she cried out, "Wait! I'm delirious that you are alive. James?" When he kept walking, she ran after him and lunged, throwing her arms around his spare waist. She held him from behind, her head buried in his back.

Praise God and pass the beer, Temperance thought as she left them alone, Lily still holding on, James letting her, while she whispered, "Forgive me," over and over.

***

I longed to remain in the warmth of the young lovers' reunion, for it filled me, at least for a piece, better than food. It was not for me to intrude so I let them be, stopping once at a distance, and taking them in a second time. They were wrapped in each other's arms, shivering or crying, I couldn't tell. And I suppose it didn't matter. Sorrow and privation had been their lot in the perilous experiment called Jamestown, but so too had joy. Were that I would be so fortunate, to find, at the very least, my own path to joy, in whatever form that might take—a warm hearth and a good book, an unscathed George, a thriving settlement I help shape, and the most elusive of all, the blessing of peace that enshrines surrender.

***

Hugh Pryse climbed onto the wooden platform of the east bulwark dressed to the nines. His brown hair, thick and shiny, was combed neatly under his green, felt wide-brimmed hat, in which he had carefully placed a black-and-white pigeon feather. His left ear was pierced with a small gold ring. He wore a linen shirt and his finest slashed doublet, trimmed with a lace collar and decorated with gold piping, glass buttons, and green satin panels. His breeches were tucked neatly into his calfskin boots. He tugged on the end of his doublet and squared up his chin. He had grown a Vandyke beard, a new style he had carefully cultivated in the last two months. He wished his mother, who had equipped him with the ensemble as her parting gift, could see him now. He prided himself on the fact that, though the third son and therefore of little consequence in his lineage, he was at least, if his mother was to be believed, the most striking in appearance. His elderly father, perhaps jealous of his son's eye-catching style, berated him constantly, which accounted, Hugh believed, for why, even from an early age, he had an incessant desire to get away from it all.

He had manned his post as usual that evening, then crept away to prepare himself, returning before dawn, primped and ready. Just before the sun breeched the horizon, he saw the Powhatans in their usual formation, up and down the river, alert to any traffic or trespass. He had become fond of them in a way, like aloof neighbors, recognizing the tall lean one that kept vigil through the night, and the cross morning riser who'd shake off his sluggishness like a wet dog does water. There was the lone Powhatan who seemed always to sit on the bow of the canoe, his head bent pensively. Or the couriers, usually men, at least one woman, delivering food and supplies, sometimes staying for hours to share gossip, laugh, or sing. He envied them their freedom, to move about, to enjoy one another, but learned that in studying them, he was able to take the edge off of his own tormenting restlessness, at least for a while.

Hugh looked inland and saw in the distance the smoke of multiple campfires, mixing with the rising mist. He could not see the forest Powhatans, as he called them, but he knew them by their voices—the leader's gruff commanding tone, the higher pitched and incessant voice of the camp know-it-all, and a chorus of young male voices that often blended in harmonic camaraderie or erupted in discordant rivalries. They made more music than the river Powhatans, chanting to the beat of the drum, rattle, and flute. Their food he knew by the tantalizing aromas that wafted his way, especially as the morning meal was prepared. He breathed in the fried corn cakes, fish, and venison, all seasoned with sweet and pungent herbs and spices he could not identify. His mouth watered for the delicious fare as his eyes teared at his cruel fate, so like a clipped falcon, alert to the outside world, but unable to fully partake of it. Though not a Bible-toting Christian, he had begun to marvel that a righteous God did not smite the pagan Indians who persecuted the settlers, most of whom professed an unwavering belief in his son. It had finally become too much for him. The natives, he'd reckoned, were there, had been there for ages, and would still be there long after Jamestown was no more.

As the sun crested the river, Hugh cleared his throat, straightened his shoulders, and from his perch shouted to the still-slumbering community that God was dead. He did this over and over until the fort was crowded with settlers, some still in their nightshirts and gowns, gawking at him in fear and amazement.

"Blasphemer!" one woman shouted at him. "Hold your tongue. You'll bring down the wrath of God on our heads!"

A soldier, dispatched by Percy, ordered him to get down. Hugh laughed at the settlers, so papery thin that a few words could blow them about in a panic. "God is dead," he shouted, each time, in response to their exhortations. When a group of children joined hands, circled, and repeated his declaration, he clapped and strutted about.

A new mother, her stomach still bloated from pregnancy, broke up the circle and chased off the children. "He's corruption, that one is. Put him in irons," she said, her bony arms accusingly planted on her hips.

"Nay, nay. The man's sick with confinement. Let him be. It will pass."

Hugh recognized the voice of the young servant girl, Lily. He did not know her beyond a familiar face. Her remarks quieted him for a moment. He did not consider himself sick, and he surely hoped his protestations were not a passing fancy. He was simply declaring a truth that had made itself known to him in the long days and weeks of the siege. "God is dead," he said aloud, this time as if stating the obvious. He said it again, to himself, and with finality. Then, he turned away from the settlers and leapt over the palisades.

When he hit the sandy bank, he cried out in joy. He was free. Behind him he could hear the lamentations and shrieks of the settlers, but that only made him laugh. Within the walls was death; out here was life. He got to his feet, brushed off the sand, and started to walk downriver. The freedom to stride in open space was so overwhelming, he chortled aloud about God's demise and his liberation. He heard a loud thud behind him and realized someone from the fort must have scaled the palisades, deciding either to join or retrieve him. Not knowing which, and taking no chances, he took off at a run. Before he had gotten but a few rods from the fort, the first arrow pierced him in the arm. He winced, but kept running. After the second arrow lodged in his side, he slowed, bent over and staggering, but still moving forward at a brisk pace. It wasn't until a dozen missiles had hit their mark that Hugh Pryse slumped to the ground. He was still alive when, shortly after, the wolves came, tearing him and his fine clothes to pieces, leaving only the contours of his twitching legs intact and unmolested.

***

"The corn is gone," Lily said.

Temperance looked up from her notes, crammed on every empty space of her last remaining sheet of paper. For ink, long gone, she mixed charcoal and fireplace soot with a few drops of water. It left a runny imprint. When it dried, the words on the page nearly disappeared. But Temperance wrote, nevertheless, not willing or able to imagine the alternative.

"There's no more corn, mistress."

"Yes, I heard you." She went back to her notes. She needed a new quill, too. But that, she mused, would depend on an alignment of two unlikely stars, a low-flying bird and a skilled marksman.

"I don't think you understand," Lily said, sharply.

Temperance put down her quill and sat back in the chair. She didn't want to hear this latest dire report. Lily had always managed to provide for them, once hauling in an enormous snapping turtle that made soup for a week, and afterward served as a nice footstool. Those days were gone, the siege putting a stop to the possibilities of any fresh meat that did not errantly wander into the fort. Still, there was always corn gruel or corn chowder or corn cakes, improved with nuts, seeds, wild berries, and garden herbs. It wasn't much, each portion barely enough to quiet their rumbling stomachs, but it kept them alive.

"We're also down to the last of the dried fish, beans, and herbs," Lily said, satisfied she had Temperance's full attention. "There's a tad bit of oil left," she held up the small decanter from the narrow side table, "and some molasses, a thimble of salt." She cupped a wooden bowl with two hands and shook it. "That's all of the acorns. Oh, but," she pulled a pouch out of her apron pocket, "James gave me some walnuts he gathered back in the fall." She smiled for a moment, cradling the pouch. "I'll not lie, mistress. It's bad."

"What about our rations from the storehouse? Surely, the fact that we are dropping like flies works in our favor." Her words hung in the air.

"James says the cupboard is bare. Those were his words."

"Impossible! We have fewer people and less food? Something is amiss. How could Percy and the council allow this to happen?" She stood up and opened the door to the outside. The cold hit her like a slap in the face. Her eyes watered against the stiff breeze and the sunlight, too distant to provide adequate warmth. A few settlers languidly walked the perimeter of the fort. No one, save Cord hacking at the ground and Spike chasing his tail beside him, seemed to be engaged in any activity. Moments before, she had been in a state of complacent ignorance. Now she was terrified. She wondered how long Lily had shielded her from the truth and shouldered the burden alone. Though it should have made her ashamed and sympathetic, it instead infuriated her. She could stand the insufferable arrogance of Percy and her impotence in the face of it. She could live without George Yeardley's companionship, and John Smith's council. But to have Lily push upon her the burden of food—that which she could not go without, and which she had no skill in providing—was the last straw.

"How long will our supply last?" she asked, her back to Lily.

"Two weeks, give or take."

Temperance tried to disguise her shock. "Then what?"

"I don't know, mistress. James said . . ."

"James this and James that!" Temperance slammed the door and whipped around, her eyes ablaze and her face contorted with fear.

Lily's mouth fell open.

"I love him, mistress."

That enraged her even more.

"Then you are twice starved."

"What do you mean?"

"Only gentlemen are allowed to marry the maidens."

"He is a gentleman in my book."

"One, like all the others, you apparently haven't read."

Temperance wished the words back, felt the terrible ache of having gone too far.

"That is beneath you, mistress," Lily said very quietly.

"The terms of marriage are stipulated in your contract of service."

"Would that you look about and see how words on paper are all but done here."

They stood in the middle of the room, the taller gentlewoman and the slight maid, their backs arched. They had never quarreled before. For Temperance, it was an unsettling sensation, as if Lily were suddenly estranged, threatening her not with physical harm but utter rejection. Temperance wanted to hold her ground but also to draw Lily back in. She realized that their argument was not so much about food, as it was a precursor to Lily's eventual separation. Not only had she lost George, she would soon lose Lily. She was instantly ashamed. She knew she had to accept James Owen or risk losing Lily. To do otherwise would essentially mean going it alone, a terrifying thought.

"We are English yet," she said, her anger spent. "The rule of law holds." She leaned against the wall.

"Wait until the last drop of—"

"And," Temperance interrupted, "even if I were to allow such a union, the council would not. They covet the maidens for their own. There are just too few of you to go 'round."

"It's not fair!" Lily shouted. "We shall run away!"

"And join Hugh Pryse?"

Lily sagged and slumped to the floor. "'Tis hopeless." She tapped her fingers against her collarbone.

"Wait," Temperance said, her eyes focused in thought. She squatted down next to Lily. "The written word, which you have disdained, may also work for you." She took Lily's chin in her hand. "It would be a simple matter to 'produce' papers establishing your James as a gentleman."

As the words sunk in, Lily straightened.

"That is assuming I can uncover something to write on. And with. Bark and blood might raise eyebrows."

Lily took Temperance's hands in her own and laid her cheek against them.

"I am spiteful and mean-spirited," Temperance said.

"Nay, mistress. You are frightened."

They sat a while longer in silence.

"I loved the books, you know," Lily said, softly.

"You have done a fine job of keeping that secret from me."

"And the learning. I was the first in my class to write my name. Teacher said I was a quick study. Three years of it, then I had to help out at home."

"It's not too late. Is James educated?"

"I don't know. I've only ever seen him using his hands, like me. I suppose I shall find out."

"You must promise you will wait a year. To be sure."

"He has not asked."

"He will. I have seen him. He is bewitched."

Lily's smile faded.

"No, no. I didn't mean that. 'Bewitched' is only a figure of speech."

"I know, mistress. It's not that." She untied her cap and slid it off.

Temperance put her hand to her mouth.

"Your hair! It takes on red."

She nodded.

"Then the weather is about to change? That is a good thing. A storm would chase off the Indians and replenish the well."

"Not the weather, mistress. It is a darkness I can't explain."

She was shaking. Temperance put her arms around Lily. "I try to speak to it and it is mute. I try to chase it off, but it hovers."

"Where is it? I will beat it with a stick." She stood and swung her arm in the air. "Is it gone?" she asked, in mock earnest. When Lily nodded, Temperance knew it was halfhearted, that whatever haunted her persisted.

"I will never leave you, mistress."

She said this with such gravity, it stunned Temperance.

"I don't deserve such devotion. Besides," she added, lightly, "James may have something to say about that."

"I will serve you with every ounce of my being."

Her throat tightened. "I shall not exact a pound of flesh."

"Even that. I promised your mother I would keep you alive. I didn't know then why I would say such a bold thing. Now I do. You must survive."

Temperance wanted to ask why her survival was so important, but Lily was already hoisting the kettle over the embers of the fire. It contained a stew of sorts, made of a handful of beans, herbs, and fish. As she gently stirred, steam rose from the pot, creating a veil around Lily. She had never looked so ethereal, or so determined.

WINTER WHITE

FEBRUARY 1610

The snow, nearly half a foot, lay on the ground like a white map. Instead of roads, there were animal tracks, clear and indelible. The settlers who awoke to the gleaming ground cover were reluctant to collect it for fear of disturbing the trails leading to the dens, nests, burrows, and warrens that might house their next meal. Men and women gathered their weapons and studied the tracks, poised for the slightest movement or discovery. Tracks appeared to halt midstride, and then mysteriously disappear into thin air, or led to numerous tunnels underneath the palisades and outside the fort. Before long, the snow was so trampled by human prints, there was very little left to save for drinking water, let alone for map reading.

From the storehouse, James Owen watched the settlers crisscrossing the commons. It looked to him like a macabre country dance. He lifted his fiddle to his shoulder, drew his bow across the middle strings, and adjusted the pegs. He launched into the lively "Old Tarlton's Song," inspired by Queen Elizabeth's favorite court clown, the legendary Richard Tarlton. The music acted on the desperate hunters like a beloved voice from the distant past. They shot up, slowly recognizing the dance tune. A few smiled, others winced, not wanting the music to trigger memories of far happier times. James's fiddling, with its searing notes and contagious rhythms, pierced the settlers like cupid's arrow. Anne Laydon dropped her knife and began to clap. Cord forgot his limp and stomped his foot on the ground, nearly toppling over each time. Spike danced on his hind legs. The hilarious sight trumped the elusive search for food. Soon, others were keeping time. Anne moved to the middle of the commons. The women, like a flock of birds, followed and quickly formed a line. The men held back, not willing to give up the hunt, until George Percy, phlegmatic, but regal, moved from the edge of the commons to the middle. There, he initiated a second line, across from the women.

Once in formation, George stepped toward Anne, who curtsied and bowed. He took her hand and led her through the gauntlet, to the end of the two lines. The couple next to them followed suit. Before long, the men and women were breaking off, gliding up and down, laughing and clapping as if they hadn't a care in the world. The pace began to quicken, faster than the traditional time of the country dance. James took heed and improvised, speeding up and varying rhythms. He sensed the need to draw from his fiddle more than just lighthearted diversion. He slid his bow downward and up, in an almost circular and flat motion, creating a deep, guttural tone. The dancers became giddy, twirling, and sashaying. James understood instinctively that between the dancers and the dance, something unique was afoot. He demanded more of his instrument, isolating one string with his bow while simultaneously drawing on the others.

It created two voices, a high-pitched lament and a low groan, speaking to both the men and women. They reacted with gusto, throwing their heads back, crying out. Merely stepping to the music would no longer hold. They took to locking arms and spinning, bouncing on their toes and skipping. Before James's eyes, the time-honored English country dance was giving way to this unbridled upstart, born in the wilds of Virginia. Through the dance, they spoke of their trials and tribulations, of their desperate need for this brief respite from the perilous and fragile nature of their lives. There may not be a tomorrow, their bodies said, reeling to the music, but there was this moment. It lasted until noon. James played until his arms could no longer hold the fiddle, until the dancers collapsed to the ground in exhaustion, and until the snow clouds, once again, moved in.

***

She had been ordered to stay away, but she would not. Her father may be the great chief, but she was Matoaka. Impatient to sneak off, she lay on her reed mat in the *yi-hakan*, waiting for the others to fall asleep. She thought again of her father's poison-tipped words, "The Tassantasses must die." At times she hated the English, for invading their land, for disrupting their way of life. Yet, they were not strangers to her, nor were they the enemy. She was drawn to the hapless people who had crossed the sea and settled at the water's edge. But she knew that even in their bumbling ways, they were a dire threat to her way of life, that certain doom had been foretold. She also knew with a confounding certainty that they were the future, and that she would be a part of it. She could not let them die in their fort, surrounded from without by her father's best men, cut off from all sustenance, and slowly starving from within. She would aid them as best she could, with a precious gift on a shrouded winter night in advance of an impending storm.

Her female attendants now deep in sleep, she gently slid out from under the warm fur blanket and crept toward the door. The fire had burned down to embers, pulsating like a living heart. She raised the bark flap covering the entrance and peered into pitch darkness. Other than the wind and the rattling of tree branches nothing stirred. Though there was scant moonlight, the snow gleamed, sparkled on the ground. She shivered as her feet hit the crystalline surface. She smelled the dense air and held up her hand to gauge the wind, guessing that she had just a few hours to complete her mission before the storm hit. Wrapped in her furs, no less than twenty rabbit pelts stitched together, she dashed to the hollowed-out base of the sycamore tree and withdrew the bundle.

The trek to the fort was well worn, even as it was partially covered by snow. She had walked it many times, in great anticipation, the first when the palisades had been built, and her father paid an official visit, toting gifts in one hand, and his prized daughter in the other. He, the great Wahunsonacock, had opened up a whole new world to her, one that she would never close, even though relations with the Tassantasses soured. It was food that had rent them, always food, or the lack of it. When the Tassantasses had forgotten their manners, failing to express gratitude, instead, demanding, even stealing corn, her father had deemed them the enemy.

The snow began to fall, earlier than she had expected. She picked up her pace, dragging her deerskin bundle behind her over the uneven ground. As the cool wet flakes melted on her hot skin, she wondered how many more times she would have to save them, smoothing over countless squabbles, and deftly negotiating tense trades. She knew she had crossed the line when she took to warning the whites about hostile attacks, those of other tribes as well as her own. What, she wondered as she paused at the tree line and spotted the forlorn fort, had compelled her to betray her people? Perhaps it was her affection for Smith, who she was told, had died. He, alone, had kept the relations peaceful. With him gone, he could neither protect his people nor appease the Powhatans, many of whom, including her father, had once held him in high esteem. Perhaps it was also the chance meeting with the English girl in the forest. Her see-through eyes had told Matoaka all she needed to know. The girl possessed the gift she herself was born with.

The wind picked up as the snow whipped around her, stinging and lashing. The hardest part of her journey lay ahead. She must somehow steal past the ring of men surrounding the fort, then manage to sling the bundle over the palisades. She prayed that theirs was a lapsed vigilance tonight, that they had hunkered down against the dangerous weather and were already dreaming of the hunt or beautiful women. Stealthy as a cottonmouth, she slid low to the ground, her bundle in tow. The wind, howling now, and the great gusts of snow, nearly blinding, provided cover. Her outstretched hand hit the wall of the fort before she saw it. She nearly cried out with relief, then, acting quickly, flung her precious cargo over the palisades.

She hurried back across the clearing, worried that she should have brought more food. But several pounds of jerky was all she could manage. Better, she hoped, was the rest, the maps of prime hunting and fishing spots outside the fort that she had drawn up on sheets of bark, and a detailed accounting of when her father's men left their posts, providing opportunities for the Tassantasses to breech the barricade and find food. In a separate letter, she recounted the vision of a great ship arriving soon to deliver them. Hope, she knew, was the greatest gift.

As she neared her village, she wondered about the part of her vision she did not relate in her letter. It was of a young man who would arrive on the great ship and take her for himself. She knew it might be the ultimate betrayal of her people, but for her, it was fate. That one day she would be known forever, not as Matoaka, but Pocahontas.

***

The bag hurtling over the palisades knocked Cord down as he was emptying his bladder. He instinctively covered his head with his arms, thinking he was under attack. He looked to his left and right and peered behind him. There was not a soul in sight, not that he could see much in the blizzard. He cursed again, this time for his bad luck. He could have pissed in his chamber pot, but he didn't want to wake his mates or add to the foul odors that permeated everything, even the very walls. He could have brought Spike with him for protection, but the dog was curled up by the low fire fast asleep. He spotted something lying in the snow, lumpy and inert. He got to his knees and crept toward it, fearing the worst. He poked it with his finger, relieved that it was not a corpse. He recognized the pelts stitched together as Indian work. "B' God," he said. "What's it doing here?" He sat on his heels and scratched his jaw, not sure whether he should open the bag or take it directly to Percy. He thought for a moment then slowly untied the drawstring, stopping every few moments to make sure no one was coming up on him.

When he pulled out the jerky, he gasped. He put it to his nose to make sure his weak eyes were not deceiving him. He breathed in deeply. Then he bit into a strip, barely chewing it before he swallowed and crammed another piece in his mouth. Oblivious to the snow covering him, he did not stop until he had devoured half of the supply. He paused when his hunger began to subside and his guilt crept in. He set aside the remaining jerky, slipping a small piece in his pocket for Spike, and vowing to give the rest to the women and children. Then, he dumped the rest of the bag's contents onto the snow. He squinted at the sheath of papery-thin bark, stacked together neatly and tied with a leather lace. It was a correspondence of sorts, he knew that much, and certainly from the Indians. Duty dictated that he take the bundle to Percy. Instead, he untied it. The wind picked up, sweeping the pile out of Cord's hands and into the air. He leapt to his feet, lunging for the layers of bark. They whipped around him as if they were taunting the lame fool who deigned to rein them in. Eventually all the sheets were blown to the four winds, all but one. Cord had collapsed in the snow when a single fragment of bark floated into his lap. He held it close to his eyes. It was a sketch of the fort, in its distinctive triangular shape. Whatever else the sketch may have detailed would remain a mystery, and haunt Cord for the rest of his life.

***

I swallowed my share of snow that winter. It was plentiful and convenient, falling to the ground and gathering, usually as we slept. We would awaken to the wedding-white present and join the others, most of whom had given up hunting illusive animal tracks and simply scooped up the snow in their bare hands and ate it. A person looking from the outside may have thought we were congregants of a newly organized religious sect, engaging in an act of communion. In reality, we ate the snow because we could, as much as we wanted. It somehow fooled us into thinking we enjoyed abundance rather than crimping deprivation. Lily fostered the illusion by adding molasses to it, creating a frozen treat. It was fresh and delicious, a balm for our empty bellies and depleted spirits.

As the weather warmed, and winter skulked away, the snow melted, returning only occasionally, in fits and starts. Though that meant spring was nigh, the absence of the snow, so pure and clean, afflicted us sorely. Its beauty alone fed us, in some ways. The dull brown earth it left in its wake seemed at the ready for little more than housing fresh corpses, the likes of which grew in alarming numbers through the winter months. Death was a monstrous mole burrowing beneath us, surfacing every so often to gorge itself on the living.

Though ubiquitous, it was not triumphant, at least not yet. On the final day of February, a single daffodil appeared. Where it came from, I wasn't sure. I was too transfixed by the brilliant yellow flower, carried triumphantly, and appropriately, by Priscilla Collins, who herself glowed with her unborn child. As she strolled through the marketplace, Priscilla held her head high and the daffodil on the green stem like a scepter. She smiled and nodded at all those who cheered her find. It was a glorious moment, full of the promise of rebirth. I never saw either of them again, not the plucked flower nor its regal bearer. To this day I wonder if what I had seen was real or a phantom, borne of unremitting hunger and deluded hope.

THE IDES

MARCH 1610

Robert Ford stood at the pulpit, gaunt and listless. He was an unassuming presence, so pale this morning, the settlers wondered if the surgeon Morton had let his blood. He appeared to be gathering his strength, weighing the import of his sermon. As a layman, he was not trained in the Anglican faith, but he had been called to take on the mantle of spiritual leader since the death of Rev. Hunt. Others had preached—the sexton, Percy, and a boy, Nate Peacock, who had a natural gift for oratory—but the settlers preferred Ford, perhaps because his reluctance to assume such a lofty position spoke to his sincerity. His scratchy voice, which sounded as if he suffered from a perpetual sore throat, added to his allure, absent as it was of bombast and self-importance. In order to hear him, it was almost necessary to stop breathing.

A gentleman with no education or skills in much of anything but etiquette and leisure, he had come to his faith after a night of drunken debauchery while a student at Oxford. Waking up in his own vomit, he remembered little about the evening, though he knew it involved a girl. He could neither recall her name nor her whereabouts, only flashes of her face, smiling in one instant, distorted and crying the next. On the floor lay a bracelet rosary, the bone beads strung with silk. In that moment, he fell to his knees and begged forgiveness, though he was not sure what, if any, sin he had committed. He spent months searching for her in the streets of Oxford, the rosary in hand, finally deciding that the only way to end his torment was to move across the sea. As an act of atonement, he practiced abstinence, and became learned in scripture. It had saved him from his unyielding conscience—until he fell in love with an Indian girl. His head had been turned by Wahunsonacock's third wife, who had attended church services on several occasions as a curious spectator. She was a beautiful and intelligent woman, and she paid flattering attention to him. Through her, he saw himself anew, no longer damned, but among the redeemed.

The silence in the brightly lit church grew. A few men cleared their throats. Empty stomachs grumbled. A little girl squirmed on the backless cedar pew and looked up at her mama. George Percy, settled in his comfortable cushioned chair in the chancel near the pulpit, put his hand on his thigh, as if ready to push off and rescue Robert from his reverie.

"God hath forsaken us," Robert began, barely audible. He clutched the lectern and kept his head down.

The nave, as if on cue, leaned in.

"He hath put us at the mercy of the Indian heathens." His voice rose, and he lifted his frail arms off the pulpit. "We are doomed."

A woman at the back of the church shrieked. Her husband,

cradling her, looked at Robert as if to say "Take care," but he kept quiet.

"Now ye must forsake God!" He shook his fist in the air. "Ye must turn your backs on the Almighty!"

Percy shot out of his chair. Robert stayed him with his hand.

"So spaketh the devil, so sayeth the devil," Robert panted, "who seduced our brother in Christ, Hugh Pryse." He lowered his arms and looked out at the parishioners for the first time. His dark eyes, black as pitch and fervor, gleamed. "We must be on guard that Satan does not take possession. It would be his great victory, his triumph in the New World."

Percy sat down, visibly relieved. Robert took in the dwindling faithful in the nave. Of the nearly three hundred settlers who had sought refuge in the fort just before the siege, fewer than half were left. And they were dying in droves. Some had even taken to digging their own graves and lying in them, waiting for the end. Robert understood how critically important God was to the survival of Jamestown. They were on the brink of chaos, their only tether to civilization a gossamer-thin thread of belief in a divine and benevolent ruler who would deliver them.

"Ye that have gone the way of Hugh Pryse, who are sore with the Lord our God, will suffer his wrath. Do not think for one minute you are safe. Wicked men will pay the price. Backsliders will tumble into the maw of hell!" Robert threw his head back and closed his eyes. In the nave, women dabbed at tears and men shuffled their feet. When he opened his eyes again, after a long pause, his face softened.

"Hear me now." He leaned forward. "We are the chosen ones. He hath delivered us this day for a glorious purpose. The New World will be reconciled with the ancient laws and eternal commandments of our Father. God hath charged us to love one another and him with all of our hearts and all of our souls. But that is not all. We must also love our enemies." He extended his arm and pointed toward the river. "They are not the devil. Remember their kindness: they have aided us and provided succor in times of need. Remember their ingenuity: they have taught us great skills in survival. We call them unregenerate who must be saved from their own ignorance and brought to the Lord. But God asks that we also listen and learn from those unlike ourselves, to delight in a peace that passeth understanding. Vengeance is his alone. To us is given the commandment of mercy. The natives wait for us, and God waits."

Robert sat down to a stunned silence. The settlers were in no mood to love the people who were starving them to death. And yet, by demanding their compassion, Robert put them squarely in control of the standoff, besieged but powerful, poised to transcend the limitations of the flesh for the incomparable throne of the spirit. They could feel large, expansive, where before they sat small and mean.

Robert had predicted Percy would likely consider it gibberish. Before the siege, the Indians were useful tools for survival; now they were a scourge whom he repeatedly vowed to wipe out, if they didn't do the colony in first. Percy quickly took the pulpit for the reading of scripture. He flipped the pages of the Bible, his large eyes on Robert. He seemed primed to redress him, but perhaps thinking better of it, turned his attention to the nave.

"God speaks to us directly from the Bible in matters of famine."

He presented the opened black book to them with a flourish, then set it down again. Robert knew that Percy had been peppered with questions from the settlers about how to feed themselves without violating biblical sanctions. They had come to him hat in hand or hands wringing aprons, seeking clarification about what would be considered unclean meat. While the Protestants had ended Catholic prohibitions against most meat, the taboos lingered, as did a natural revulsion to eating certain of God's creations. Percy had summoned Robert, ostensibly to confer on the matter for the upcoming service. But, in a rare moment of contrition, Percy confessed that he, himself, had become lax in studying the content of the meals his steward, Ralph, prepared. Nor would he ask. "The time has long passed," he had said, "when being an epicure is either fashionable or prudent." And now Percy appeared resolute, armed with scripture, no less, to address their burning questions.

"In Genesis nine three," Percy said, his long finger pointing to the chapter and verse, "God says to Noah, 'Every moving thing that lives shall be food for you.'"

He shut his Bible and sat down.

***

Lily followed closely on James's heels. She carried a bucket and a makeshift net while he held a hoe and a stick, which he used to poke through the mud puddles. Occasionally he would mash his heel into the muck, hoping to roust out a potential meal in hiding. Rain still fell, as it had for three days straight, but it was light and the air was unusually warm. Crickets and frogs announced spring in their syncopated rhythms. It was a maddening concert; the settlers who still had the drive and energy to search for food could hear their prey, but they could not see them. When they got close to the chorus, it stopped instantly. At any other time, when they would not have been starving, the young lovers may have laughed and marveled at the sly creatures. But hunger kept them single-minded.

"There," James whispered. He pointed to a rotten log lying against the palisades. They tiptoed over to it and spotted the greenish-brown frog, neatly blending in with the moss. Though it was overcast and there was no threat of her throwing a shadow that might scare the frog away, she knew to act quickly. She dropped the net, made from the muslin of a discarded dress, on top of the frog. Then, she gathered the muslin and frog with her hand, dropped the frog in the bucket, and closed the lid.

"That's one," James said. He was as slender as the stick he carried. His golden wiry hair had turned brown and dull over the winter. "Wait!" He held up his hand and listened. He circled around the end of the log, raised his hoe, and chopped down. She heard a thrashing noise. James jumped backward. "Christ," he bellowed, shaking his hand.

"You're bitten!" Lily gathered a clump of mud and pressed it on his hand. "Hold it there."

She took his hoe, approached the riled snake, solid black and about four feet long, and, with one swift blow, decapitated it. It writhed until she finished it off, chopping the body in two.

"It is not fatal. There were no diamonds on its back. Your hand will swell but you will heal." She held the two pieces of the snake. "Here," she said, offering him one.

"Nay." He shook his head, holding his injured hand by the wrist. "What kind of man would take food out of a lass's mouth?"

"You found the snake, James. Here."

She could see he weighed the logic of her argument, then

took his half from her, and stuffed it in a deerskin pouch attached to his belt.

"I should be providing for you, Lily," he said.

"There are many ways to provide."

He started to walk away, keeping his hand elevated.

"Wait!" she said. "How do you cook it?"

He shrugged. They looked at each other, reduced by hunger to little more than rag dolls with straw hair, and began to laugh.

"We are a pair," Lily exclaimed.

"Are we?" he asked, bounding back toward her.

She lowered her eyes. He took her hand. Where hers was rough and chaffed from chores and constant labor, his were still relatively smooth for the hands of a man who worked with wood as well as played it.

"Marry me," he said.

She dropped her chin and shook her head.

"There is the impediment, I know. Only gentlemen marrying," he said. "There are ways around the settlement rule."

She pulled away.

"Well then. You find me repugnant?"

"Nay, nay, beloved. Your face is more beautiful to me than . . ." she grasped for words. "This!" She held up her portion of the snake. "Which we do not know how to eat." They laughed again.

"The snake got the better of it!" James said, shaking his swollen hand.

"Yes. It died with the sweet taste of your flesh in its mouth. I should be so fortunate." She smiled, flushing at her own boldness.

He pressed against her, smelling of shaved wood and sweet musk. He kissed her in plain view of the settlers milling about. They seemed not to notice. "Then say yes," he said.

She nodded. He threw his head back. "Io to Hymen, now the day is come," he began to sing. "Uncover thy head and fear no harm."

"Shh! James!"

"I don't care!"

"We will have to wait a year."

"A year!" he cried. "We could all be—"

"Don't say it. I promised mistress I would wait a year."

"You both were so sure I would ask?"

"Mistress knew before I did."

"She is a very wise woman. Perhaps," he said, winking, "she will know how to cook the snake."

"On that count, you would be wrong."

"I am the proudest man alive," he said.

"Stay that way, my beloved."

"Proud? Of course."

"No. Alive."

***

As the weather turned and spring emerged so did the vermin, which surely sniffed out the scent of death in our fort, and knew we were ripe for the picking. But we were not dead yet, not all of us, and the vermin landed more often in our pots then we did their bellies. I admit to turning up my nose at first, fending off the foul pottage Lily stirred with the intensity of Macbeth's witches. She had silently dismissed my fastidiousness, then eaten the mess, gray and lumpish, as if it were the finest capon. When I realized a day or two later that such fare would be the norm, I ladled my helping onto my plate. It was not revolting—whatever it was, since I never again asked Lily to identify the contents of our meals. I ate it, and I was glad, for my stomach—at least for a few hours at a time—was sated.

That is what hunger does to you. It has been years since I suffered the terrible agony of starvation, but it stays with me, as much as a scar from a life-threatening wound. As a way to put the constant craving for food out of my mind, I began to compile in my head the characteristics of starvation amongst the settlers. Many, of course, died, as hunger ate away their sinew and muscle and fat, eventually leaching the bones before working its way to the organs. By the latter half of March, just as the air turned sweet and the swamp willows bloomed, we had lost all but eighty people. Those that were left comprised a most sorry spectacle. Work had ceased. The marketplace was a haunt, as there was nothing to trade. The forge's cheerful clanging became silent. The few farmers left, scratched at the ground. Soldiers gamed, but as there was little or nothing to wager and no drink to whet their whistles, the usual boisterous comrades were as somber as penitents. The women fared better. Hungry or not, there were still beds to be made, floors to be swept, clothes to be laundered, food (such as it was) to be cooked, children to be groomed and schooled, men to be coddled.

Amongst the general malaise, there were common themes. The bodily humors were all out of balance, wreaking havoc on the settlers. As they wasted away, their hair turned brittle, skin dried, and complexions were sapped of color. Gums bled and teeth rotted, even in the children, who began to grow strange bellies. Constipation was rife, and many forgot to replenish themselves with water. The women did not bleed but it hardly mattered, as the men lost carnal interest. Even the most stalwart and forbearing were listless but quick to anger, weak but prone to sudden bursts of nervous activity. They talked but struggled to make sense, heard but did not listen. Settlers stayed to themselves, foregoing even the respite of church fellowship. And these were the more mild effects.

As for Lily and me, we also succumbed to some of these baleful tendencies, but for the most part were spared. Lily managed, with ingenuity, fortitude and, I suspect, a strong stomach, to keep us fed and away from the abyss into which so many were tumbling. But it was not long before the supply of snakes, frogs, turtles, mice, and rats was exhausted, when there was nothing left to eat but air.

***

Henry Collins hung from the scaffold by his thumbs. On his feet were attached heavy stones. Lily thought he looked like a Christian martyr, with his thin blond hair draped across his face, writhing in pain, and his slender body clothed in little more than his threadbare nightshirt. He was no martyr, though. Lily knew it, had known it for a while from the series of sensations she'd felt whenever he was near. She had found, to her dismay, that as her hunger grew her visions became more varied, no longer restricting themselves to just portents of the weather. Now, she had the ability to read people. At times, she wasn't sure if she were clairvoyant or delusional, gifted with divine intuition or just faint. And yet, what she felt from people was always accurate.

"Aye. I knew that bumfodder were up to something," she heard a soldier brag to his friends. "He get caught stealin'? Can't be much left in the storehouse worth stealin'."

"Dunno," said another. "Most likely he was pilfering someone's stash. Probably Percy's. He's hoardin', he is. Knob-nosed eunuch."

"Quiet, Balloch!" said a third, an old man cupping a hand to his ear. He had tended the horses at Jamestown. All had been eaten. "He'll be confessin' shortly. Don't fart ar you'll miss it." The men guffawed as Henry screamed in agony. "Percy's made good use a this contraption. He's the third scoundrel this month what's been put on the rack."

"Did you hear about Cord?" Balloch asked.

"Nay," said the soldier. "The farmer?"

Lily braced. She hadn't seen or heard from him in days.

"Aye. 'Twas the worse sort a scum did him wrong."

"Hie! Tell me before I knock yer brains out. What happened?"

"It were Spike."

"Nay. His dog?"

"He found the carcass. Weren't nothing left even the buzzards could pick at. I never seen a man so aggrieved. Cried 'til he fell asleep, right there next to his dog's bones."

The men said nothing. Lily felt sick. She had eaten her share of vile creatures, but she had not resorted to butchering pets. Cats and dogs, so vital to the colony, had all but disappeared.

"That's low," the old man said. "Were it Collins, do you think?"

"Dunno."

"Where's that pretty young wife a his?" the soldier asked. "If he's guilty, he's done for. I wouldn't mind squirin' the likes a that one."

"The only way she'd have you," Balloch said, "would be roasted in garlic and rosemary with an apple in yer mouth."

Lily stepped away quickly from the grim humor before her nausea got the best of her. She had come to bear witness to Henry Collins, to discover what her premonitions foretold about the young man whose only other offense had been an actor's love affair with the sound of his own voice. The men gathered for the spectacle knew as little as she did why he was being pilloried. She did not know how much longer she could listen to his screams of pain and thought she might instead seek out Priscilla, who probably was in need of comfort. Something told her to stay put.

"I did it! God help me, I did it," Henry wailed. "Get me down. Please. Let me loose."

The official in charge of the torture, Tom Wylie, did not move.

"Confess all before God and your fellow men, Henry Collins," he said, loud but without conviction. "Ere I loose you, ye must confess."

"Yes. Yes. But undo my thumbs. That at least."

Tom released his hands, sure the weights on his feet would keep him grounded. Henry slumped to his knees.

"Make haste," Tom groused, eager to be done with it.

Henry rubbed his throbbing wrists. He had no intention of dispatching his story quickly. He waited for the crowd to swell and for their anticipation to reach a breaking point. Only then did he hold forth, delivering his final monologue.

"It was her fault," he said. "She was with child. It is shocking, forsooth. When she told me, smiling as if she were the Virgin Mary, I nearly took a puke. But, heed! 'Tweren't mine. I hardly touched her. It was her father, 'his accursed fatal hand / That hath contriv'd this woeful tragedy!' The man was the devil, draped in God's disguise, and she was his concubine. A nasty business, father and daughter. She became an affront to me, her womb the nest of the spike-tailed demon. As her belly swelled, so did my terror. Nightmares visited me. I could not sleep next to her and took to the floor. She begged and pleaded with me, the sugar-coated tongue of the fiend. I was not fooled. When she thought I was unaware, I saw her yellow eyes and the cleft foot.

"At supper last night, she was convicted. I caught her licking the blood of the serpent. ''Tis for the baby,' she had said, but I knew better. I held her by the throat to expose her forked tongue. She wrested loose and ran for the door. 'Beware the Ides of March,' I cried out, and withdrew the knife from my scabbard. I hesitated and doubted. The fiend had shifted. She was once again my fair delicate wife, a mirror image. I could no more harm her, than myself. As I lowered the knife, she reached out. I spied the claws. The guise had slipped. I screamed 'Speak, hands, for me!' and plunged the knife into her breast. I watched as her foul breath became ragged and her yellow eyes rolled into her head. It was not until the final violent spasm that I knew the demon had left her body.

"I longed to weep for her, but I knew to act in haste. I quickly opened her stomach and cut out the devil's spawn. Under cover of night, I tossed it over the palisades into the river."

The onlookers witnessing the confession backed away from Henry. The crowd let out a noise like those wounded and left on the battlefield.

"For God's sake, man," Tom Wylie said. "Where is Priscilla? What have ye done with her?"

Henry smiled but said nothing. Tom Wylie kicked him in the gut, then in the head. Henry held up his hands to ward off the blows. When Tom reared to kick him again, Henry yelled "Stop!" He cradled his head and rocked.

"Speak or I'll cut out yer tongue," Tom said.

Henry lowered his arms and lifted his face to the crowd. His hollowed-out eyes bore into them.

"God gave me permission. Percy said as much: 'Every moving thing that lives shall be food for you.'"

Several women began to whimper. One fainted. Others, including the soldier and his mates, were bent over retching, expelling from their empty stomachs the purest form of bile.

THE BEATITUDES

APRIL 1610

Henry Collins was executed, hung from his neck until dead. His heinous crime, subsequently recorded in George Percy's report, was made great sport of. Black-hearted wags opined how best to prepare a wife for consumption. I suppose they meant in their crude and insensitive humor to deflect the savagery of Henry Collins's act, to restore to him a measure of humanity. But, in so doing, they stripped Priscilla of hers. A sweet and kind young woman whose goal in life was to serve God, she was thrice violated, by her husband's unspeakable brutality; by his confession in which he publicly impugned her virtue; and by Percy's report, which does not even deign to mention her name. Whilst in print and lore Henry Collins comes off as something of a resourceful rogue, dispatching two irritants at once—an empty stomach and a disagreeable wife—Priscilla is reduced to grist for the comic's mill, an amusing footnote to a sordid history.

To us at the time it was hardly a laughing matter. Henry Collins not only murdered his wife and unborn babe, he became a cannibal. His behavior, though roundly condemned, and punished, had brought to the fore what lurked in the settlers' minds during the darkest days of the Starving Time. Murder was a mortal sin, but what of natural death, and the resultant bounty that might pertain?

***

James Owen lay down his bow and fiddle. The last strains of "Lunatic Lover" had left the dark quarters of his mates, and drifted, he hoped, across the commons to Lily's bed. He had not sought out this dangerous mission, but watching Lily waste away before his eyes was motivation enough to risk his life to feed her. Percy had called for the expedition shortly after Henry Collins's confession. It was said that it was not Percy's fear of rampant cannibalism that compelled him to take action, but rather the threats of a certain young gentlewoman to expose one day, both publicly and in print, his lack of fortitude in quelling the flesh-eating in its tracks. His decision to send any and all able-bodied men to hunt and gather was much belated, and most certainly would be fatal, but it was, nevertheless, a chance.

James reached for the pistol lying on the table and shoved it in his belt. He strapped his fiddle to his back. If he were going to die, he wanted it with him. The musket he took from the bracket above the fireplace. He was the last man to leave the cramped space, ushering the others out the door before dawn with music. He had feared rousing the men with the mournful lament, especially Richard Lyle who he was sure would smash his fiddle to smithereens. The expedition warranted some pomp, some ceremony. The men had sat up in their cots, sluggish from sleep and hunger. They listened pensively, their heads slung low. James had barely begun when he heard a beautiful bass accompany him. It was the cooper. James's fingers slipped on the frets, but he quickly collected himself. The bald-headed bully sang sweetly about an unfaithful woman whose deceit destroys her lover. "*See how the pale fool doth waste?*" he crooned, his hands crossed against his heart. James marveled as tears streamed down Lyle's face, traveling along the deep gash in his cheek. Richard Lyle had not hated James's music. He simply could not bear to listen to it. Whatever memories haunted him, they had kept his golden voice mute—until now.

James fetched his canteen and supply of powder and shot, hurrying to join the men already gathered in the commons. Halfway there he spotted a rare sight, a few sheets of curled bark strewn along the underside of the palisades, barely visible. It gave him an idea. He gathered them, hoping one might do. All three were in roughly the same condition, thin and fragile. Each, to his surprise, contained a drawing. He chose the driest and most supple for his purposes, and, in a rushed attempt to pocket the other two, crushed them to pieces. With the remaining sheet of bark, he jogged back to his quarters where, with only the stub of a pencil left to his name, he gingerly crafted his message. This he left for Lily.

When James finally arrived at the commons, Percy had just finished his rallying cry, though by the looks of it, the handful of bedraggled and starved survivors was in no mood for empty platitudes about valor. Percy lingered a moment or two, the men's silent response quickly driving him off. Captain Martin, their leader, nodded to Robert Ford, who stepped forward and blessed the expedition, his burred voice infused with a nervous excitement. James noticed he was dressed and armed for the expedition. No man, not even the puny Ford, James mused, could be spared.

"Preacher, ye going with us?" Balloch asked, incredulous.

"Faith, I have been called," he said. The musket he held was nearly as tall as he was. He seemed confused about how to carry it, lifting it by the barrel. James took it out of his hands and placed it against his shoulder, then positioned his hand under the butt.

"I see ye got yer farting-crackers on!" Balloch pointed to Robert Ford's breeches. "You'll be fillin' 'em up apace." He cackled.

"Leave 'im alone," Richard Lyle said. "If he's got the stuff to go out there,"—he jerked his head toward the gates—"he's alright with me."

"Aye," Balloch said. "Then it's on you to save 'im when the heathen buggers got his arse in the air."

Robert Ford shifted the heavy musket to his other shoulder, nearly dropping it.

"We'll not get fed standing here whilst you run your clappers," Captain Martin said. "We've got all of an hour 'til dawn. After that, we'll be fish in the barrel for the Indians. Be sure and paint your faces. Red and black." He passed around several chunks of charcoal and a bucket of red clay diluted with water. "Hunt in pairs and keep your wits about you. Use the knife and net as best you can. Don't discharge your weapons unless it's to defend yourselves. But remember: one shot and you'll have the Indians aplenty, like fleas on dogs." He paused and looked at them, not like the sorry lot they were, but like the fourteen-year-old son Martin had lost in his first year at the settlement. He longed to go with the men but Percy forbade it, the settlement leadership already severely reduced in numbers. "I've faith in you," he said. "Snatch as much as you can—fin, feather, hoof—and come back alive."

They moved in a line toward the northern wall and climbed

over the fence stealthily as skinks, lifting their legs gingerly over the spiked logs of the palisades. They slid down the other side, then stopped and listened. Darkness still covered them, but only for a short while. The men paired up quickly. Before James knew it, he stood alone with Robert Ford. He swore under his breath. Those rogues had planned it this way, he was sure.

"Well, then," he whispered. "Let's get on with this." He held his gun at port.

Ford ignored him. His black eyes gleamed oddly. He wasn't afraid, James surmised, more so feverish and excited. Ford took the lead, walking rapidly upriver, his posture erect and his gun tight against his shoulder. James hurried after him, scuttling close to the ground.

"Robert," he snapped, "take heed. Stay low and mind the noise."

Ford gained steam, marching ahead, as if he were nearing a battleground. He tripped and stumbled over all manner of underbrush, creating a ruckus. But he kept on.

"Damn it, you fool!" James said. "Be quiet or you'll get us killed."

Ford broke into a trot. Without warning, he swerved from the river into the forest.

James ran after Ford, hoping and praying the Indians on the river were asleep or oblivious. When he hit the tree line, he saw Ford's gun, lying on the forest floor. Ahead, through the trees, he caught a glimpse of Ford's back. James hesitated, confused. The preacher was headed straight toward the Powhatan village. Other men had deserted to the Indians, but during peaceful times. Then he realized—it was the Indian woman. She had beguiled Ford. It would be suicide. She was a wife of the chief. The randy goat would be skewered and broiled for entertainment. James cursed his fate, picked up Ford's musket, and raced after him.

The frail Ford eluded him, running with the strength and energy of a madman. James made chase, quickly exhausting what little reserve he had left. Just as he was closing in, the forest opened up. In the clearing sat the village, quiet and serene in the gray light of dawn. James had never seen an Indian village before and was struck by how English it appeared. The tightly constructed homes made of reed and bark were situated in a well-designed grid. There were several neat and tidy gardens newly plowed and ready for planting. What looked like Powhatan's home, stately and grand, sat near a rectangular meeting house as large as a country church.

James hid behind a giant oak on the boundaries of the village, hoping to spot Ford. He felt his heart in his throat. He wished he could turn around and go back, leave the preacher to the mercy of the Indians, and live to see his precious Lily again. But he couldn't. Ford, like most of the Jamestown survivors, was slightly out of his head. If James could find him before the Indians did, he would knock him in the head and drag him back to the fort. He strained his eyes in the emerging light, then heard with a sickening certainty, the familiar rasping lilt of the itinerant preacher.

"Dearest, I am come!" he cried, his arms raised in the air. He stood in front of the spacious home in which the great chief most likely slept. "I surrender to you!"

James's only hope was to reach Ford before the Indians awoke. He prayed they could not hear his wispy voice, or perhaps mistook it for an old man's nightmare. James closed his eyes, took in air, and charged ahead. A song, "The Lunatic Lover," coursed through his head as he ran. He could hear Ford, beseeching his beloved. His voice, the song, his own heartbeat—all pulsed in his brain as he lunged for Ford. It was too late. As soon as he grabbed onto the frayed sleeve of the preacher's shirt, the circle closed around them. Indian men, women, and children curiously studied the crazed lover and the wild-eyed fiddler, while from the grand estate, Chief Powhatan, cross as a wet cat from this rude awakening, emerged.

***

Lily shot across the commons past the settlers, who ambled about like reanimated corpses in search of a more suitable final resting place. She cradled in her hands James's brittle note, which she had discovered attached to her door with a brad. "I shall gather the first mushrooms of the season, a fine sturgeon, and the sweetest honeysuckle to perfume your hair," he wrote, signing his name with a flourish. On the other side of the note was a faded image, a map of some sort. It meant nothing to her but she was sure it would interest her mistress. She ran, though her legs, weak from obscene hunger, gave and bent like reeds. When she saw the men clamoring back over the wall and through the gates, she froze, her grip on the note so tight, it shattered like thin ice.

Of the dozen or so who had gone foraging, half stumbled into the fort, breathless, their clothes ripped and torn, their lives saved by the grace of God, or dumb luck. Lily's eyes went from one to the other and back to the palisades, searching for James. It would be so like him to arrive last, she thought. When Captain Martin closed the gates, Lily collapsed.

***

"They're playin' with us, they are," Balloch said. He sat on his haunches, hands on his hips. "The savages let us get so far, close enough I could smell fresh mint for the picking. I could see the fish leapin' and splashin' in the river. There were a squirrel, close as ye, mate," he pointed to a haggard soldier about six feet away. "It were all cat and mouse." He shook his head. "When we drifted too far from the fort to make a proper run for it, and we was spread out, they ran at us. Whoopin' and hollerin' and pickin' us off like deer."

Temperance cradled Lily in her lap. She pressed a wet rag to her forehead, which was hot to the touch.

"The others?" Temperance asked.

Balloch rattled off the fatalities.

"What of James Owen?" she asked. Lily stirred.

He shook his head.

"Who was he with?" Captain Martin asked.

"Robert Ford."

"Christ!" Martin said. "You let those two fend for themselves?"

Balloch chewed at a thumbnail.

"Then they could still be out there," Temperance said. "Alive."

"Aye," Balloch said. "And I'm a kelpie."

"Mind your mouth," Martin said.

"What about the food?" Anne Laydon asked. She was skin and bones. The baby she thought she had been carrying months before had been a phantom. Her garments hung on her once ample frame like tattered drapes.

Balloch held up empty hands.

"'Tis Holy Week," she said. "My mother would have already put her order in to the baker and butcher for the hot cross buns and leg of lamb. I can smell them now, the cinnamon and rosemary, the sizzling fat, and, oh, risen bread."

"Be still, woman, with yer holy rubbish and yer sotted memories," Balloch snapped. "Easter is a grim farce, don't ye see?"

"Devil!" Anne cried, shaking her head and walking off.

"The fronds," Lily said. She struggled to her feet.

"Lily?" Temperance asked, helping her up.

"If I lay the fronds, he will return," she said, and stumbled about collecting stray branches laced with leaves.

"Jesus would no more show up in this pisshole than King James himself!" Balloch said.

"Lily, Lily, no." Temperance reached for her. She jerked away and dropped her small bundle. She crumpled to the ground and hung her head. Temperance gathered her up, led her home, and put her to bed.

***

It was then I became the handmaiden and Lily the mistress, though had she been well, she would have chafed at our switching roles, as if the servant were a more exalted status than the master!

I see in retrospect she is correct.

Tending to the sick and aggrieved is an art form for which I had little aptitude. After I tucked Lily in, she slept for a full day and night, waking only briefly, in a delirium, to condemn the absence of fruit on the trees. When I assured her it was yet too early in the season for fruit, she shook her head, as if I were the dunce in the corner. She quickly fell back asleep, waking again in the wee hours of the morning. I heard her thrashing and stood over her not sure what to do. Poor thing, she had to instruct me in how to tend to her. "Water," she whispered and pointed to the ladle in the bucket. I held it to her lips, but managed only to dribble the water on her. She said, "Help me up, mistress." I did as I was told, holding her head and back with one arm and anchoring the ladle with the other. This time, she got a good drink, and lay back down.

Again, I stood over her, blind to her needs. I picked up a book and read aloud. I thought she might fall asleep. Instead, she waved her hand as if the words were gnats pestering her. I covered her shivering body with a blanket, which she promptly kicked off. It was only when I felt her feverish forehead and held her ice-cold hand that I sensed relief. To provide comfort, I had simply to sit with her.

Day passed into night and neither of us had eaten a single morsel. I knew she needed sustenance, but she had always been the provider. I had no idea where the food we ate (what little there was of it) came from or where it was stored. I did suspect she had for weeks stinted herself of her fair share. I knew it, and in my greed, allowed it. Now in my shame, and fear of losing her, it was I who would go without. I prayed to God it was not too late.

I got on my hands and knees and searched every crevice of our small home. Not a sliver of food was to be found. I was tempted to lick the floor near the hearth, for spillage, then thought better of it. I scoured the outdoors around our building, collecting leaves and sticks, mud, in the pockets of my skirt. None of this was edible, though it somehow made me feel better. I searched the storehouse. There was naught but dust and cobwebs. I would have taken the spiders, had they not already been plucked. Exhausted, I determined to return to my quarters. I passed Janus Hobbs, near my age but looking like an old man. His eyes were sunken, his mouth worked like he was reciting the rosary, though he was no Catholic. I saw that he wore stockings without shoes, his feet caked in spring mud. I should have been sickened by the sight. Instead, I was buoyed.

When I returned home, Lily was alert, but senseless. "It is the end of days," she said, lying on her back, her arms crossed over her chest. I tried to reassure her, as the healthy tend to do disingenuously, that it was her fever talking. Her words chilled me to the bone. She was fast for the grave and I was not far behind, if I did not soon conjure nutrients. I quickly set a pot to boil over the searing embers of the fire, then removed my shoes. I took my scissors and a sharp knife and cut the leather cover into pieces. These I dropped into the water and waited, until the leather was soft enough to chew. I sampled two bits before offering Lily a portion. When she swallowed several pieces, I nearly cried. She slept well that night, as did I, no worse for the wear, and with at least one pair of good English leather left to get us through another day.

***

Matoaka covered her ears against the man's din, and with her eyes beseeched the third wife, Ponnoiske, to end the misery. They stood at the open window of the chief's spacious *yi-hakan* looking out on the dismal scene. The doomed white man stood upright in the yard, lashed to the wooden post, his incessant lowing for that which he could not have, muffled by the moss stuffed in his mouth.

Any other man would have been flayed the moment he had trespassed, days before, deigning to disrupt the chief's restful sleep. And so Wahunsonacock had been inclined, sleep-deprived and fuming. As he told the story to Ponnoiske, he had made his way through the corridors of his *yi-hakan* to the front entrance. There he had witnessed the most bizarre spectacle, two white men whittled away by hunger, one pining loudly for his third wife, the other striking up his fiddle, apparently in a vain attempt to distract from the fool. Wahunsonacock had ordered them to stop. In the ensuing silence, the chief had shook his head and very softly, laughed, and then, laughed harder. Had the chief been irate rather than amused, had he been jealous rather than proud that the white man lusted after his wife, Robert Ford and James Owen would already be dead.

"You are too tender-hearted," Ponnoiske said to Matoaka. She had once been as kind as Matoaka, and, she thought, even more lovely. She still considered herself a beautiful woman. Though her skin had lost its youthful suppleness, her hair shone like polished agate, improved by swirls of gray. Her eyes, large and oval, had deepened to the color of mulled cider. But her hold on her husband, like all the women he married, was tenuous and fleeting. His waning interest had etched lines in her forehead and sharpened her tongue. "The English have turned your head by calling you princess," she taunted. "There are no princesses among Powhatans. And there is no such a one named Pocahontas."

Matoaka glowered at Ponnoiske. "You make sport of the poor Englishman long after my father has grown bored with the game." Ponnoiske felt the sting of her words. The third wife did not consider herself a bad woman, and they had once been close confidants.

Ponnoiske said nothing. Robert Ford had become her pawn months before this most brazen declaration of love. His fawning from the pulpit had flattered her at a time when Wahunsonacock had become smitten with a ravishing young woman. When her husband took little notice of the lovestruck minister, she flirted with the idea of satisfying Ford's desires. He was not to her liking, but she coveted his ardor when her own marriage bed had grown cold. An affair would slake her carnal thirst and perhaps ignite her wayward husband's. It was an enormous risk. While other Powhatan wives could enjoy occasional affairs, the chief's wives were strictly forbidden from such sexual dalliances. If caught, she would be cast out, a death sentence. Robert Ford, then, could neither serve her as lover or foil. His sudden arrival in the village had given her hope of rekindling her husband's interest, but the week-long protestations of love had become unbearable, an echo of her own unrequited love and subsequent rejection.

"Ponnoiske," Matoaka pressed. "The minister suffers. My father—"

"Your father's head is buried in yet another bush. He will not return for days."

"He has given you the power over this man's fate."

Ponnoiske laughed. Her husband merely wished to wash his hands of it. He had placed her in an impossible situation. The only power she had was to decide if Robert Ford's suffering would last minutes or a lifetime. The minister's moans rumbled through her like thunder.

"Enough!" she shrieked through the window. "Enough! Enough!"

Robert Ford, hearing her voice, grew quiet. Ponnoiske stepped out into the yard. A group of women emerged. One carried a basket of shells, several others armfuls of kindling, which they arranged at Robert Ford's feet. Another Powhatan, a young man with a snake tattoo on his shoulder, dragged James Owen into the yard. James gripped his fiddle by the neck. Behind him, a white-haired elder carried a lit torch, raised in the air.

"By God," James Owen cried out. "Have mercy." He turned in a circle, his eyes darting from one impassive face to the next.

The women went about their business methodically, meting out the shells and stacking the kindling at the exact height, just under Robert Ford's soleless boots. As if on cue, the women stepped back. The oldest and most stout of them polished her shell with her thumb. She moved purposefully toward Robert Ford.

"Put him out!" James Owen shouted at the women. "Do that at least." He turned to the third wife. "Who has loved you as he has?"

Ponnoiske felt the fiddler's truth wash over her. She looked again at Robert Ford. His eyes, though glittering and senseless, were fixed on her. He made a wretched gurgling noise, it sounded like her name. For a moment, she loved him too. She felt Matoaka rest her hands on her shoulders. Ponnoiske raised her arm to the Powhatan guard with the snake tattoo. He lifted his war club and, hesitating a split second at the apex of his swing, swung the club against Robert Ford's head.

***

James Owen fell to his knees. He reached for his fiddle and rested it on his shoulder. Turning his back to Ford, he closed his eyes and positioned the bow above the strings. For the first time in his life, the music would not come. He redoubled his efforts, waiting patiently for the right tune, the perfect dirge. But all he could hear was the sound of shells scraping against flesh. He lay down his fiddle and bow and pressed his forearms against his ears. He did not know how much time had passed before he felt the heat of the blaze at his back.

***

Captain James Davis plucked the meat from the crab with his knife and savored its salty sweetness. He tossed the shell in the bucket near his feet and reached for another on the large wooden serving platter. He was joined at the open-air table by a dozen men, their beards flecked with the delicate white meat and their lips and fingers wet from the briny juices. Tonight they dined on crab, tomorrow it might be oysters, clams, or sturgeon. When they were sick of fish, they could select a plump pig from their herd and roast it whole on a spit. Davis, rotund and pink-skinned, found himself thinking ahead to the next meal and what treats awaited him. The planting season was right around the corner, but for now Fort Algernon at Point Comfort, just thirty-two miles downriver from Jamestown near the mouth of the Chesapeake, enjoyed a surplus of food.

As the men ate, the only sounds were the cracking of soft shells, moans of delight, and intermittent belches. They could not excavate the morsels fast enough. The men ate with the gusto and relish of those who do not take serendipity for granted. James Davis understood all too well their good fortune. He had flirted with deprivation on his first voyage to America several years before, while taking command at Fort St. George, where the Popham Colony was founded on the far northern reaches of the Atlantic coast. After a brief stay, he had opted to leave the colony early on, surmising that they had arrived too late to plant crops, and that their eventual desperation for food would soon vex the native Abenakis to no good end.

When he returned to Popham from England months later with a resupply, his hunches were confirmed. The colony, which had hoped to exploit natural resources for profit, had failed to do much of anything besides survive. The Abenakis had turned their backs on the colonists, and even the Popham leader, Raleigh Gilbert, stepped down, announcing his return to England after learning he had inherited an estate there. With no one eager to succeed him and the prospects of another brutal winter, the likes of which the English colonists had never experienced, they decided to call it quits. Davis escorted them back to England in the one grand accomplishment of the colony—a pinnace they had built named *Virginia* that not only crossed the Atlantic safely, but would sail again when Davis joined the Third Supply bound for Jamestown.

Had it not been for the Powhatan scout he and his lieutenant, Richard Fenton, had cornered while hunting in the forest just before Christmas, he would not have known they were besieged. "We must rescue them," Fenton had said. He was a stout young man, with thick black hair that would not stay combed. He wore no beard, and so was as open and honest in appearance as he was in deed. Davis found his lack of guile both annoying and useful. He could trust Fenton explicitly, but he also suffered vague sensations of guilt around him. Fenton, he told himself, had read too many romances. He fancied himself a knight. Davis had no such illusions. When he was a boy, he had brought home a stray cat, infested with all manner of filth and vermin. His mother had screamed at the sight of the bedraggled animal on her newly imported Persian rug, boxed his ear, and immediately sent him to his room with no supper. The episode had cured him of heroic inclinations.

When young Fenton called for them to liberate Jamestown, Davis recoiled. "We are duty bound to this post. Deserting it would be the death of all of us," he had said. "The Indians most surely are lying in wait. Better we hole up until May when the natives will be preoccupied with spring crops. It will be our opening." Davis remembered the look on Fenton's face. It shamed, then infuriated him. "Don't be stupid, man! We are no good to Jamestown if we are dead." Fenton had resigned his commission the next day. It was just as well. Davis had no intention of ever setting foot in Jamestown again. Come spring, he and about a dozen other men at Fort Algernon planned to load up the two pinnaces docked at Point Comfort and sail back to England. He took a large swig of ale from his cup and rested it contentedly on his paunch. He regretted the Jamestown debacle, but it was time to cut his losses. There would be other, better opportunities in this golden age of exploration. He knew his contemporaries would judge him a heartless mercenary, but he was sanguine that history would be kind.

***

George Percy sat across from John Martin at the long cherry table in his quarters, his thin arms stretched before him and his palms flat. The two men were the only members left of the original council. They were joined by Richard Crofts and Henry Adling, both gentlemen who had sailed in 1607 with the first wave of settlers. The words they spoke came slowly, almost painfully, in part because they were starved, and because they were stricken by the nature of their proposal.

Percy, who listened as Crofts argued the merits of the case, had just that evening eaten the last of his starched ruff. He struggled to concentrate. He had taken to hearing voices, of his mother, deceased settlers, even John Smith. He saw ghastly phantasmagoric faces rush at him in his bed at night, and sometimes as he walked about the commons. At times, he would smell the aroma of a fresh-baked apple pie or the savory juices of a crown roast. The scent was so strong, so real, he would lick the air. He wondered for the hundredth time how he had gotten into such a predicament, and what had compelled him to abandon his comfortable life back in England. Ambition for honor and power were always the answers, but they did not fill a dangerously empty stomach.

"So it is," Crofts concluded. Percy realized he had not heard a word he said. Nor did he need to. He knew the gist of it.

"And no gentlemen will be disturbed?" Henry Adling asked. It was a rhetorical question, and so, perfunctory. Adling was perhaps the most handsome man in the fort, tall, well-built, olive-skinned, with green eyes. He had managed somehow to remain immaculate, his black beard and pink nails trim and clean, his clothing fresh and neat. Women swooned over Henry Adling, but he was particular, not eager to take any of them for a bride though he, as a gentleman, was entitled to.

"Noblesse oblige," Percy said.

"Be steadfast, Percy," Adling said. "It is for the best. We must survive. It is the only hope."

"How do we proceed?" Crofts asked, raising his eyes, a light gray turned blue by cataracts. He had a thin layer of black hair, like that of a newborn baby, and wore a spare pointed beard so that he appeared quite naked, almost obscenely so. Percy disguised his sudden urge to retch with a polite cough. John Martin shot out of his chair and left the room.

"You will need to employ the laborers, and perhaps soldiers in case there is resistance." Percy looked out the window like a condemned man in prison. "The surgeon will be instrumental."

"A butcher would be more to the point. Does one still breathe?" Adling asked.

Crofts scratched his head. "The last one perished with that fool, Pryse. 'Tis lamentable but not insurmountable. I would not hesitate to perform the deed, if necessary."

"We will need to act quickly, within a day," Adling said, "as to avoid spoilage."

"Of course," Crofts nodded.

"Good God," Percy cried out. "And would you haggle over the finest cut?"

"Pray, do not allow your delicate conscience to weaken your resolve," Adling said. "I think only of England."

And your stomach, Percy thought. He had already prepared a mea culpa, which he would include at some point in his reports back to investors. That way, he would render powerless the meddlesome Flowerdew, whose veiled attempts to blackmail him into a ruinous mission nearly wiped out what was left of the fort's able-bodied men. Still, he knew his preemptive admissions would do little to assuage the collective horror of a civilized society.

"If we perish," Crofts added, "Spain and France will control the New World. We would be greatly diminished."

"So it is that we sacrifice the lowly?" Percy asked.

"So it has always been," Adling concluded.

***

I had not wanted to leave Lily that night. She had insisted, filled with a strange light that frightened me. "Please, mistress," she had begged, "tend to the others. They suffer and are in need."

We had spent a quiet two days together, I reading to her about ocean currents or sailing routes, which, oddly, she had requested. It calmed me more than it did her, but she seemed not to mind the long seafaring passages. Her delirium had abated, and she came and went in sleep, calling out to her mother or James, chastising the moral shortcomings of our feckless leaders, reminding me to do this or that, all of which I obliged. I prayed the fever would break and she would soon return to me.

I thought my prayers were answered that night when all of a sudden she awoke, full alert, sat up and pointed to the hearth. "There," she said, indicating a brick not quite flush with the rest. I pried it loose and found inside a packet. I cried out when I saw the corn cake, dry as the brick that concealed it, but as welcome a sight as I had ever or since beheld.

I sat on the edge of Lily's bed and broke it in two. We ate the cake, her slowly without enthusiasm, I with the hunger of a ravenous beast.

"I will sustain you," she'd said.

"So you have."

"And so I will." She took my hand and looked me dead in the eyes. There was no mistaking her intent. I quickly withdrew my hand and stood up.

"Why? Why has it always been me?" I asked. "Are you not as worthy of life?"

"It no longer holds me, mistress."

"I cannot live without you. It is too cruel."

Lily smiled, as a mother does with an anxious child.

"You and I are of a piece."

She then asked me to leave her and tend to Jane Ashton, whose feet were covered in boils, an affliction for which there appeared to be no cause. I did not relish the task and at first demurred. "Nay, mistress," she'd said smiling, "'tis for your own good." When I continued to resist, feigning incompetence in such matters, Lily rose up and begged me, as if it were a matter of life and death. I left her, reluctantly, and knocked at the door of the poorly Jane, surrounded by her two children, a boy and a girl, and her husband, Jacob, all of them white-blond, pale, and thin as marsh reeds. The smell of infection nearly sent me out the door, but I heard Lily's voice in my head, and held fast. When I put Jane's feet in a tub of hot water and gently bathed them, she sobbed. I felt my uneasy stomach settle, and my chest expand. After Jane was comfortable, her feet wrapped in clean rags, I turned to little Bess and John, scrubbing their be-grimed faces until they gleamed. I clipped Jacob's hair, which had reached his shoulders, then swept the hair clean. I had saved a few crumbs of the corn cake, most of it what Lily would not eat, for the little family. They chewed slowly, as if it might last longer that way. Before I left, I put the children abed and listened with a strange gratitude and wonder as they recited their prayers, thanking God for many things, the last of which was me.

***

Lily waited to hear the latch catch, then eased herself out of bed. On all fours, she crawled to the table and pulled herself up, relieved to see the small bundles. Temperance had done as she was told, carefully wrapping the seeds Lily had harvested from the fall garden in wet rags for germination. She feared planting them before the last frost, but she had little choice. Her hands, shaking and thin as claws, grasped the seed packets. She looked again through the open window at the full moon. Its hypnotic light guided her toward the door, gave her strength to venture out. She saw to her delight that Temperance had again followed her instructions perfectly and prepared in the last few days the small garden bed by hand. The soil, thick and loamy, was carefully tilled and fragrant. Lily nearly cried. She had not thought she would smell the earth again.

There were four rows to be sown, each about six feet long. Lily gathered her strength and got down on her knees. Temperance had assured Lily she could plant the seeds as she had been taught. But Lily knew there was more to gardening than skill; it required a bit of magic. Mistress would scoff at such nonsense; Lily lived by it. She planted one seed at a time, pushing her finger into the damp soil, then placing the seed vertically. She covered the seed with a thin layer of dirt before moving on to the next. When she was finished, she raised her arms to the moon, and in a tremulous voice, like that of a novitiate, made her offering. She stretched out next to the garden, laying her head on her frail arm. Before her heart stopped, she saw, in colors more vivid than any she had ever experienced, a pulsating green of a stately flower's stalk, and the luminous white of the sacred bloom.

***

Cord was awakened by hisses outside his window. He shook his head free of sleep and listened intently, so as to make sure he was not dreaming. When he heard the unmistakable hissing again, he rolled out of his cot, lifted his musket and, fighting his trembling hands, managed to load it. He slowly opened the door of his quarters realizing once again that Spike was not at his heels, would never be again. He fought back his grief and crept out, his eyes not needing to adjust much in the bright moonlight. He looked left and right trying to locate the sound, then spotted the turkey buzzards, two of them, on either side of the prize they were vying for, which Cord could not make out. He stayed low to the ground, fascinated by the hideous birds, their featherless red heads and ivory beaks much too small for their large black bodies. They flapped their wings at each other and charged halfheartedly, as if hoping to expend the least amount of energy to secure the contested meal. Cord raised his musket and aimed it at the noisiest one, his arms shaking from the anticipation of fresh meat. Just as he was about to squeeze the trigger, he heard heavy footsteps, of men giving chase. Cord cursed as he watched the buzzards fly off, his best and perhaps last chance at food. In a fury, he pointed the musket at the dark shapes of the men who had scared off the birds. Henry Adling and Richard Crofts, skulking about in the night like ravenous wolves. He would have blown their heads off, suspecting that out of all the remaining settlers, they were the most likely to have butchered and feasted on his dog. But he hesitated, startled by what they did next.

On the ground, lying as if she were asleep, was Lily, gleaming like a toppled obelisk in the moonlight and just as lifeless.

"Crofts!" Adling whispered. "Here."

The two of them bent down and peered at her.

"She's the Flowerdew maid," Crofts said.

"Aye. It's a hard loss. Her mistress will be sorely aggrieved."

"'Tis providence," Crofts said. He picked her up and draped her across his shoulders. He was none too gentle, but Cord was relieved that they had managed to spare Lily the gruesome fate of the buzzards, or a disfiguring shot. He lowered his musket and fought back tears. She was a fine lass through and through. He had loved her in his own way. Tomorrow there would be a burial, once Mistress Flowerdew got the news. As for tonight, he had lost twice and sorely, the chance to eat and a stalwart maiden.

***

Temperance closed the door on the Ashton quarters and glanced up at the moon. It shone so brightly it hurt her eyes. She looked away to the stars, forming shapes in the sky that the ancients had been compelled to name. Temperance scoffed at such efforts, which she felt reduced the magnificent to the familiar. A bear, an archer, a harp, a queen. Constellations were not comforting mirrors of earthly realities; they were the ciphers of the universe, which stargazers had not been able to properly translate. She wondered what they said to her now, to them, to Jamestown. They were so distant yet filled the night sky with their brilliant light. Surely she and her fellow settlers were not meant to die in the midst of such immense beauty and intelligence. Yet here they were, skeletal remains of cosmic abundance.

As she walked across the commons, she thought of Lily and smiled. To Lily it was simple. The world would turn on its axis, and human beings must tend to their business. The great ontological mysteries would never be solved. There were always beds to be made, and gardens to till, meals to cook, children to be raised, lovers to caress, and the old and sick to tend to. Those moments, the culmination of a day, a year, decades, were all that one needed in understanding the purpose of life.

She remembered the seeds Lily had instructed her to plant and felt an eagerness that surprised her. The prospect of an ear of corn or a pot of green beans made her heart skip a beat. To be able to grow her own food out of the dirt amazed her. In her previous life, which is what she called it, food was delivered to her on a silver platter. She had little idea, nor did she care, where it came from or what it took to prepare it. Tilling the garden in preparation for planting seeds had made her feel powerful in ways that acquiring knowledge did not. With something as insignificant as a seed, she could feed herself, she could survive, if she could just last long enough to reap what she sowed. To that end, she had made a momentous decision. She would read once more her most trusted source on Virginia, Harriot's book, cobbled together painstakingly after the vile Bruce ripped it apart. Then that, too, would be sacrificed, the pages tinder for another fire, and the carefully tooled leather of the cover, at least one more meal.

Nearing her quarters, she looked at her handiwork, the small garden waiting, like a woman in her marriage bed. Yet something was different. She noticed that the soil had been disturbed in an orderly fashion. When she spotted the rags, she knew. Lily had preempted her. She laughed out loud. "Praise God. She is not so sick she cannot put in a garden. I shall scold her for her impatience."

She hurried into the darkened quarters, then stopped short. It was empty. She went back outside and searched behind the building. Fear took hold of her and she called out softly in the silence. A screech owl answered her. She rushed back to the garden. When she saw the imprint of a body in the sandy soil, she cried out. A hand touched her shoulder.

"Lily?" She jumped.

It was Cord. He shook his head. The moonlight lit the silver streaks in his hair.

"No." She pushed him away with such force he nearly lost his balance. "No!"

He told her he was sorry.

"Be still, fool! She's about. My Lily." She cried out her name, three times. She doubled over. The long strands of her dark hair fell out of her cap into her face. Cord put his arms around her. She fell against him.

"Where have they taken her?" she asked.

"To the graveyard, methinks." He brushed her hair out of her eyes. "Crofts and Adling."

"What?" she asked, straightening. "They are strangers."

"Aye. But they saved her from the buzzards."

"Those two wouldn't save their own babes."

She broke from Cord's arms and ran toward the small plot reserved for the dead. There she saw the two men at the grave's edge holding a long plank. She was weak, from grief, from not eating, from the short run, but she managed to call out. The men dropped the plank and turned to her. They parted when she got near. Temperance knelt down and touched Lily's cheek. She lifted her hand and kissed it.

"We were covering her, mistress," Adling said. "The board and weights on top would protect her remains, until tomorrow and a proper burial."

Temperance ignored them and beckoned Cord, who had followed her. Together, they gently lifted Lily out of the grave. Cord took Lily in his arms and carried her like a baby.

"You had no business," Temperance said. "She is my girl."

"She must be buried," Crofts said to her retreating back. "At first light."

Temperance left the men in silence and led the way back to her quarters. She had Cord lay Lily in her bed, then dismissed him. She stripped off Lily's clothes and threw them in the fire. She cried out when she saw her frail body, her fat and muscle nearly gone, her lucent skin barely concealing her bones. Temperance heated water and washed Lily's hair. With a rag and crude soap made from lye, she bathed her slowly, taking note of her delicate fingers, the scar on her kneecap. She pared her nails and buffed them with a bit of coarse stone. As her hair dried, she drew from her own trunk her finest nightdress, spun from silk and never worn. Temperance had been saving it for her wedding day. She lifted Lily by the shoulders and shimmied the gown down the length of her body, careful not to let her tears stain it. She slid satin slippers onto her feet, then combed and braided her hair. With her fingers she dabbed a bit of lavender oil, which Lily had pressed one summer before, behind her ears. There was no lily to place in her hands, so Temperance settled for a sprinkling of wild violets in her hair.

Satisfied, she clasped her hands and knelt beside the body. She had stopped crying. There was stillness in place of the wracking sobs. Lily would not like such a demonstration. She wanted to pray but to whom or what stymied her. Her father in heaven and the martyr on the cross were at this moment, in the presence of this simple maid, too overbearing. Lily had lived a happy but uncelebrated life of servitude and had died peacefully without violence and spectacle. None would start a movement in her name and only a few would remember her. Yet Temperance found herself wanting to pray to, and not for, her. It became the seed of what she had never expected would happen, the beginnings of her own salvation.

***

When John Martin finished the scripture, a verse from Psalms, Cord positioned the wooden plank, the only semblance of a coffin, on top of Lily. That done, he thrust his shovel in the loose pile of dirt and tossed it into the grave. He had filled it about halfway when the dark clouds rolled in from the south. The winds kicked up and thunder shook the ground. Temperance clamped her hand down on her hat lest it fly off. The few mourners who had attended the brief funeral scattered when lightning flashed into the James River like a celestial tributary. It took the ensuing rains to drive off Temperance, a downpour so swift and powerful the fort began to flood before she could make it back the short distance to her quarters.

It rained for a good half hour, an assault of thunder, lightning, hail, and winds. She crouched under the table and read Harriot one last time, though she couldn't comprehend a thing. When the storm subsided, and the brilliant midmorning sun reappeared, she ventured out. The gates, which had been wrenched open by the storm, were quickly closed. The grounds were flooded, layered in mud, and strewn with all manner of debris. Emaciated settlers picked through the mess, hoping to find a hapless animal or bird caught in the effluvia. The graveyard appeared to have been erased. The crude wooden crosses marking the graves were washed away as were the neat divisions between gravesites. She splashed through the standing water to Lily's grave. The plank that had covered her rested on a mound of mud. Her body was gone.

***

My report grows long, purposely so, for I have protracted it to avoid this moment in history. I warn you that this entry doth offend, there is no detour. Your every sensibility, belief in Christian virtue and human decency will be unmoored. But this is not my intention. To the contrary, I hope to enliven the meaning of sacrifice, to release it from liturgy and biblical scripture into divine praxis.

It came to pass on Easter Eve and the traditional lighting of the fires. Of the two hundred or so settlers who had inhabited the fort before the siege, only sixty were left, and of those perhaps thirty well enough to join in the celebration. The fires were meager, the settlers not having much wood left to burn after the trying winter. But they were determined. Ritual was all they had left, what they clung to as a symbol of their shared humanity. As the fires burned brightly, the weathered pine of dismantled buildings going up like tinder, the settlers sang psalms and recalled memories of past feasts. Their eyes, sunken and tortured, reflected the light of hope from the cheerful blaze. It was a wonder to see, those wasted souls who surely would not last a fortnight, mustering up the will to spend what little time they might have left in fellowship.

Cord walked amongst us, balancing a large platter, covered with linen. He came to a stop near the arc of settlers standing near the largest fire. When the settlers had concluded their song, he drew off the linen, revealing a large portion of shaved meat. The settlers gasped and clapped. "Yer a wizard, Cord," the Scottish soldier, Balloch, said. "How'd ye do it?" Cord smiled sweetly and shook his head. The look about him was sodden with grief and resignation. We met eyes, for an instant, and I knew. The shock was twofold, at the utter horror and perfection of the offering. I had been foretold by her in word and deed but had refused to see. Cord beckoned the settlers, who lined up one at a time for a sliver of manna. "Take it and eat," he said, with such solemnity I hardly recognized him. Ere long, the platter was nearly empty. I had not selected a piece, could not. Cord approached, his uneven gait causing him to rise and dip like a gull riding the crest of a wave. "No," I said. "It is defilement." Cord's face flushed with blood and his lips quivered. "Nay, nay. The human vultures defiled. This, what I have salvaged, we consecrate."

He held out the last bit to me. I knew I had to, else it would be for naught. I closed my eyes, prayed to God for my mortal soul, and took what was left of her.

***

Under the cover of darkness, James Owen slid from one tree trunk to another. He had perhaps minutes to reach the fort before daybreak and so hurried as best he could without making noise. When he spotted the east bulwark, devoid of a sentry but intact, his heart pumped with such force, it propelled his body forward, throwing the cautious workings of his mind to the winds. He tripped on a thick vine and crashed headlong into the underbrush, making nearly as much racket as a felled tree. He waited in the ensuing silence, for the Powhatans, whom he knew would be on him in minutes, if not seconds. Time passed torturously slow. In the utter blackness, he bemoaned his fate, having managed up until now to stay alive in the Indian village by making clever use of his music. After the lay-preacher had been flayed and torched, James had been certain he would be next. But he misjudged the Powhatans' love of music, no different he supposed from the English, and instead of execution, he was commissioned to compose songs in honor of Wahunsonacock. The third wife, Ponnoiske, also took a sudden interest in the fiddle, demanding a lesson. The only tune she cared to learn, and the one which she played and sang once a day, was "Lunatic Lover."

Like a troubadour in the king's court, James performed for Wahunsonacock every evening during his supper. Several times he had joined in various celebrations, adding the stringed instrument to the flute and the drum. The women were smitten with the

Tassantass who made love to his fiddle. Yet, James kept his distance from the maidens, out of faithfulness to Lily, and to appease jealous suitors, any number of whom stood watch. Soon, the guards learned to trust him and became complacent. On this night, James waited for their evening chatter to wind down and the chorus of snores to commence. He seized his opportunity and ran. Now, no more than yards from safety and his Lily, he lay on the ground defeated, a victim of his own rash and clumsy behavior. He put his hands to his aching temples. He waited, but still the Indians did not come. There were no sounds coming from the fort, and no movement in the bulwarks, as if the settlement had been abandoned. The sun's halo lit the sky. James stood on wobbly legs and listened. He heard nothing but doves and quail breaking news of first light. He ventured out from the forest and scanned the river. There was not a single canoe or raft to be seen. He whirled around and faced the tree line again. It was utterly still, undisturbed by the chortles or footfall of Indians. The siege, James realized, had ended.

He raised his arms and shouted. He started to run but, dizzy from the fall, he nearly toppled over. He slowed to a fast walk. Just as the sun crested the river, he saw her, outside the gates of the fort. "My love," he cried out, "I have returned to you. We are saved!" She held out her arms and embraced him. James pressed his forehead into her shoulder and wept. He seemed not to notice that she was naked. He kissed her, holding her head with his hands. He smelled the violets and sweet scent of her luminous skin. "I shall never leave you again," he said, looking into her clear eyes. She smiled. "Come." He let go her hands to throw open the gates. When he turned back to her, she was gone.

The brightness of his smile evaporated. He called out for her, his fearful shouts turning to hoarse screams. Temperance rushed out in the damp morning air in her nightdress and fastened herself to the fiddler. He tore at her arms when she gave him the news, but she held tight until he fell to his knees in exhaustion. When she tried to help him up, he stopped her with his hand and slowly rose. He lumbered across the commons and disappeared into his quarters. Moments later, the forlorn thrum of his fiddle flooded the compound. He played all Easter Sunday and every day after, his music the dirge the settlers needed to commemorate the loss of so much and so many.

THE RETURN

MAY 1610

Thomas Lark cast his net in the James River. A lad of about ten, he had stopped talking the day back in February when his mother had to butcher Chester, his beloved cat. He refused to eat that night, or to speak. As if silence were fertilizer, he grew uncommonly tall. He tried to coordinate his ungainly arms and legs, in order to fling the net effortlessly, as he had been taught by his father. But he couldn't quite manage to toss it so that it landed flat. Inevitably, the net folded or twisted. He tried again and then again. Finally, he got it right and peered greedily into the black waters for it to fill. As he hovered, a sudden surge of the current pushed him back. Before he could regain his balance he got hit by another. He looked up, squinted, then went rigid. "Ah! Ah!" He pointed, though he was alone, and swiveled his head, looking for someone, anyone, to tell. There being no one in sight, he splashed to shore like a sea lion, barking stupidly and flapping his arms. Ross Lark, a head taller than his son, took him by the shoulders and shook him.

"Be still, Tom, and speak sense. What possesses you?"

"Ships, father!" His voice was hoarse from disuse. He seemed startled by it.

Lark darted out the gate, along with several onlookers who had heard the commotion. At the water's edge they saw it, the gleaming white sails of two ships like a starched cornette gliding toward them. The men threw their fists in the air shouting hurrahs. They were soon joined by the other settlers, a sorry sight, survivors so weak they could barely stand, so dried and shriveled from want they could not shed tears, and so hopeless they did not recognize hope even when it filled them.

Temperance pushed her way to the front of the crowd and felt her heart race. Anticipation roiled her stomach. The ships could be the territorial Spanish or filled with marauding pirates. They could be the French or another load of passengers come to increase their already impossible burden. But something told her it was none of those threats, that this arrival was the blessing they had waited months for. She shielded her eyes from the bright May sun and strained to see any signs or markings of the ships' origin. She paced the shoreline, growing excited beyond measure. Finally, amongst the settlers' anxious murmurs and near hilarity, the roar of the strong breeze, and the cacophony of bird calls, she recognized a sound she had never expected to hear again in her lifetime. It was George Yeardley, her George, announcing from the lead ship's forecastle to all those gathered, in his slightly comical and pretentious way, that the wayward leaders of the Third Supply had, at long last, arrived.

CHRISTMAS

ANNO 1628

Temperance had barely touched the Christmas goose, cooked to perfection by Darcy's rum-soaked husband. She suffered through Francis's guests, two boorish councilmen and their wives, who droned on as if their life stories were epic adventures. Anxious to return to her report, she felt nausea as the feast was laid before her, not able to eat the roasted pig, cheeses, pies, and her favorite, white bread. When she excused herself, before the pudding was served, her loquacious guests seemed scandalized.

As she lumbered up the steps to her chambers, the baby kicked in her belly with a malicious urgency. She knew it would not be long before it would see the light of day.

George barely recognized me. I had been diminished by half while he was robust and hearty, as were the settlers stranded on Bermuda, all 150 of whom had survived, living quite well on the bounty of the island. Rumored to be a hellish place, it was quite the contrary, offering an abundance of fruits, nuts, fish, and roots in a climate as temperate as a mystic's repose. No wonder that George was in the pink of health and no worse for the wear. I saw the shock in his face when he beheld me. It was a true barometer of what I and the rest had suffered. I pressed my hands to my mouth, not wanting him to see my poor neglected teeth and swollen gums, yet unable to suppress an ecstatic smile. He took my hands away, drew me to him, and kissed me full well in front of all gathered. There was laughter and back-slapping, more hurrahs and sporadic jigs. And there was food.

The Bermuda contingency had been resourceful and industrious. Not only did they live off the land, they put supplies by. They could have set up their own colony on the paradisiacal island but their fealty was to England. They procured food to deliver to Jamestown and fashioned two ships, Patience *and* Deliverance, *out of the bones of the dashed* Sea Venture. *We ate that night, and a few nights afterward, filling up on salted fish, dried fruits, and fresh crabs, transported in pipes filled with saltwater. With so much at once, many of us took a puke—a wanton waste—then ate more.*

When the three-day celebration came to an end, the new leader of our fragile group, Sir Thomas Gates, surveyed the wreckage of the fort and declared the settlement a resounding failure. We were to pack up and leave immediately. That might have been the end of Jamestown, a short and dismal chapter in English and American history, had it not been for yet another miraculous turn of events. Halfway down the James en route to England, we encountered Sir Thomas West, the Virginia Company's newly appointed governor. His ship was laded with settlers, and food sufficient to revitalize the deserted colony. Amidst not a few protestations, Sir West promptly circled us back to Jamestown. That night, as we all acquiesced, for better or worse, to the permanency of our fate in the New World, George Yeardly proposed to me. I accepted, of course, for I could not refuse a man who deigned to survive against all possible odds. It boded well for our future.

"M'lady." Darcy poked her head in the door. "'Tis good to see ye smiling."

"Fond memories, Darcy."

"Was the food to yer liking?" she asked. "Ye barely ate."

"Superb. Especially the goose. Jim knows his way around the kitchen."

"Aye. That and the pub."

They laughed. Darcy studied Temperance.

"I can stay with you tonight, if ye like."

"No, no. Go home to Jim. It's Christmas."

Darcy nodded and shut the door, quietly. It frightened her, Darcy's sudden solicitations.

She pushed herself away from the escritoire and stepped into the long hall. She could hear the guests in the parlor, where they were still holding forth and most likely imbibing a small fortune of sherry, chocolates, and nuts. She made her way to Francis's room and found him kneeling by his bed in prayer.

"What is it that you ask for?"

"Ah! Mama. You scared me. I thought you were a ghost!" His hair was a mess of dark curls, which Temperance threaded with her fingers. "I asked God to send Papa to me on Christmas."

Temperance drew him close. He pressed his head against her extended belly.

"Does the baby peck at you like the chicks in their shells?"

She laughed.

"I am not an egg, Francis. I have a womb."

He thought about that deeply until his sister's voice from outside the door shook him loose.

"Argoll! Give that back!" Bessie shouted.

Francis ran out in the hall. Temperance followed slowly, cradling her stomach with her arms.

"Mama! Argoll has taken—" Bessie darted to Temperance, tossed her long dark braid over her shoulder and put her hand to her mother's ear. "He has taken my garter and threatens to give it to Harry!"

Argoll, hiding around the corner at the end of the hall, dangled the garment so that it appeared to be doing a disembodied jig.

"See!"

Temperance clapped her hands sharply. Argoll peered around the corner. His large brown eyes flashed remorse.

"Give it to me."

He walked it to her, holding it at arm's length. She took it and balled it up.

"I shall be the one to present this Harry with said gift."

"Mama! No!"

Bessie looked at her mother in horror. The two boys were thrilled. Temperance held them like that for a second, then flashed a wry smile.

"Oh!" Bessie gasped in relief. "You tease!"

The boys burst into laughter. Bessie and Temperance followed suit.

"You," she pointed to Argoll, "must be your sister's greatest advocate." He nodded impatiently having heard this many times before. "It is a man's world. Make it less so." She turned to Bessie. "Marry well or not at all. There is no in between. And you," she gathered in Francis, "must be—"

"I know, Mama. I must be of service. Because I have a big heart!" He put his hands to his chest then threw them outward.

"Yes. And because it is the way and the light."

The house quickly chilled as the hearths burned low. The guests, still eating through the governor's store, were quiet, their voices reduced to a simmer after hours of roiling.

"To bed now. I have work to do."

"Your writing, Mama?" Bessie asked.

"Yes." She felt her heart lurch. She had not thought her daughter gave two wits about her writing.

"Am I in it?" Bessie asked, her eyes wide.

The boys repeated her question.

"No. None of you was born yet."

"I shall write, too, Mama," Bessie said.

"Remember me, daughter, when you do."

She ran her hand down Bessie's braid and touched her cheek. When she reached for Argoll, he twisted away, protesting the intimacy. Francis, as if to make up for his brother's rudeness, squeezed her so tightly, she yelped.

As they returned to their rooms, she watched them until they were behind doors. She listened for the groan of their beds, the sweet music of their modest prayers, and the sighs, signaling relief from whatever burdens they carried, imagined or real.

For nigh on sixteen years I have lived on the sandy edge of this verdant frontier. Like George, I, too, am something of a living miracle, having survived famine, sieges, and numerous

Indian raids, the worst one the 1622 Powhatan attack in which nearly a quarter of the English in and near Jamestown were slaughtered. I have birthed three children, lost my indefatigable George prematurely, and now confront the prospect of my own mortality. In the face of such trials, I have not only been favored with relative longevity but matchless opportunity. I am a woman who has enjoyed the liberties of men, and a fortune of her own. After George's death, I inherited a one-thousand-acre tract of land, which he named in honor of my family, albeit more modestly, the Flowerdew One Hundred. The plantation yields a handsome profit from sundry crops and resources, but mostly from tobacco. With it, I oversee the men and women who work the land, a responsibility I do not take lightly. After all, it was George and I who were among the first to purchase Africans for servitude. As their numbers have increased, so has untenable legislation against them, which has threatened to stain the moral fabric of our settlement. Slave labor has proven quite lucrative and tempts even the most upright amongst us. Were I to live another score, I might make amends. As it is, I must leave it to my children to do what is right, hardly an easy task.

Outside of the plantation, I have achieved a measure of esteem in the public sphere. I witnessed the will of a true luminary, John Rolfe, a dear friend whose genius in planting the first tobacco crop insured the commercial success of Jamestown and the English presence in the New World. His wife, Pocahontas, I met only briefly. But we were kindred spirits, she and I. We shared a laugh once about Sir Walter Raleigh and his purported gallantry in laying his garment across a puddle for Queen Bess to cross.

"If this man washed clothes as women do," Pocahontas had said, her ebon eyes flashing, "he would have kept his breeches on." Had she lived, I am certain she would have done much to repair and improve relations between her people and ours. She had a knack for diplomacy that is sorely lacking—nay, devastating. I fear the time has passed when the Indians and English can live together in mutual respect. The Indians suffer the worst of it.

My contemporaries have treated me with uncommon respect, but posterity, I know, will not be kind. I shall not be abused or defamed, per se, merely neglected. My husbands' grand accomplishments will be fully noted and recorded, especially George's, whose life is storied. Among his myriad triumphs, he made peace with the Chickahominy Indians in 1616, which allowed for a period of equanimity and calm. He was knighted by the King, appointed governor of Virginia, and convened the first legislative assembly right here at the Jamestown church. Flowerdew thrived under his stewardship, which included erecting the first windmill in Virginia. Heaven knows what else the man could have achieved had he not died at forty. I do not begrudge dear George his just rewards, only his early demise. I am deprived of him as is the community he helped found. Whatever accolades historians confer upon him, he has earned them. I do not seek any for myself. I have no appetite for fame. Still, I wonder what goes missing when the women are nowhere to be found as actors in history. It is but half of the story.

So it is I write, for Lily. An Englishwoman newly bloomed in a harsh and unyielding landscape, she chose service, not conquest; care for others not personal gain. When the settlement teetered on the edge of collapse, she did not welcome death as a form of escape, but as a means to an end. Her willingness to give of herself so readily in the manner she chose, and for us to accept her gift, challenge the very foundation of civilization. Lily did not die for us as Jesus did, to take on our sins. Lily's sacrifice exemplified our virtues, which we could draw on to ensure our survival. I am fully aware her selflessness is not unique. Mothers, as do soldiers in battle, give all to others. But she is unique in that she chose not just to serve her own children or her country or her earthly masters. Her mistress was humanity.

Temperance lay down her quill, got up from her chair, and slowly descended the steps from her bedroom. The house was quiet, the guests long gone. She saw a dim light pulsating under the door of her husband's library but passed him by. The smoke from pipes and smoldering embers hung about like invisible webs. She opened the front door and stepped out into the frigid air. The snow fell about her shoulders and gathered in her hair. She felt the peace of this moment. She raised her eyes to the heavens, teeming with flakes, and gave thanks, to God, to Jesus, and this other. A girl named Lily, a nobody who became everybody.

ACKNOWLEDGMENTS

How fortunate I was to have been raised by a mother and father whose home was filled with good books, abundant laughter, and oodles of kids. Seven brothers and sisters to be exact, all of whom have been unflagging in their support of my decades-long, pie-eyed dream. The greatest gifts my parents ever gave me were my siblings: Kirk, Dyke, Karen, Kris, Diane, Holly, and Sarah.

There are the Heinze non-bloods, long-suffering of our clannish idiosyncrasies and always encouraging of my endeavors. To Katha, Phyllis, Paul, Steve, and Ken, for whom the distinction "bloods" and "non-bloods" has ceased to exist.

And then there's Deb, who reminded me time and time again that it is always darkest before the dawn, even, and especially, when life seemed filled with endless nights.

To Julia Livshin, my agent. My editor, Corinna Barsan. And Haila Williams, acquiring editor at Blackstone. What a superb team. I could not have envisioned a better trio of professionals to guide me. I am also grateful to copy editor Ember Hood for her careful attention to detail, to publicist Hannah Ohlmann for her hard work in getting the word out, and to Zena Kanes for her gorgeous cover design.

I drew on numerous sources to recreate Temperance's milieu, including firsthand accounts, documentaries, literature, and histories, especially *A Land as God Made It* by James Horn, *Jamestown, the Buried Truth* by William Kelso, and *The Jamestown Project* by Karen Kupperman.

Finally, many thanks to my readers—Molly Draney, Kirk Heinze, Donna Lee and Al Frega, Karen Heinze, Kris Marnon, and Sarah McKay—for providing honest, insightful, and often detailed appraisals.